RUN
for your
LIFE

JANE
MITCHELL

Little
Island
Books create waves

RUN FOR YOUR LIFE

First published in the USA in 2023

First published in 2022 by
Little Island Books
7 Kenilworth Park
Dublin 6w
Ireland

© Jane Mitchell 2022

The author has asserted her moral rights

A British Library Cataloguing in Publication record for this book
is available from the British Library.

Cover illustration and design by Wajeeha Abbasi
Typeset by Tetragon, London
Printed and bound by CPI Group (UK) Ltd,
Croydon, CR0 4YY

Print ISBN: 978-1-912417-85-8
Ebook (Kindle) ISBN: 978-1-915071-29-3
Ebook (other platforms) ISBN: 978-1-915071-28-6

Little Island has received funding to support this book from the
Arts Council of Ireland / An Chomhairle Ealaíon

10 9 8 7 6 5 4 3 2

There are over two thousand young people in Ireland living in Direct Provision centres. Some of them have grown up in them. Some have lived out their childhoods waiting for a decision about their futures. They've had to put their lives on hold, unable to fulfil their hopes or dreams.

If you are one of them, this book is dedicated to you.

Chapter 1

'My ghosts are whispering to me,' Mother says.

She hears ghosts whispering in the air as clearly as I hear my sister's soft voice and my little brothers' laughter in the evening air. I believe her. Ghosts and spirits have always whispered to Mother or walked in her dreams. Women in our village at home used to visit her to find out if their sick cow would live, or whether they should start preparing for the funeral of an old mother-in-law.

She smiles at me now. There's sadness in her smile as memories bubble to the surface. Her sadness swallows me up and I wish I could turn back time.

It seems my life has been split in two, as different as lemons and mangoes. The first part was in our village back home, so far away. My memories are mostly warm and bright: my sister Sharnaz, my brothers Kashif and Musa, our friends Iman and Ruba. School and sunny days. Some of my memories are dark and frightening: my father and the village council, leaving school. Having to run for our lives. Mother mourns life in our village – her husband and children, her home, her friends. She frets she made bad decisions.

'Things should have been different,' she tells me.

The second part of my life is in Ireland, as different a place from my home as you could find. It's all about new things, new places, new experiences. Some are exciting, most are difficult. My only constant is my mother, and I am hers. We cling to each other like two people drowning. We cling to each other because we have to.

Mother can't get used to life in Ireland. She can't get used to being away from everything she has known. Her body is here but her heart and soul were left in our village. It's been so hard for her when all she knows are the hot and dusty streets. The mango trees and jasmine flowers. The washing stones by the river. There are many things I miss from home, but mostly it's the people tearing at my heart. Now, I shiver at Mother's words. Her ghosts always tell of something bad.

'Your ghosts never tell you good news, Mother,' I say. 'They never announce happiness or joy. They only ever see darkness or danger.'

Mother shrugs. 'They are ghosts. They see what they see, Azari.'

.   .   .

It's the end of summer when we arrive in Ireland. White men in uniforms find us hidden among huge boxes and containers on the ship. Bright beams from their torches dazzle us as we crouch in the corner among empty food packages and bottles and blankets. The men shout. More come running. I think I hear English, but I'm not sure. The voices are loud, the words fast and confusing. They pull us out. Mother struggles to get to her feet. I'm crying. Trying to get away but there's nowhere to go. Fresh air. New smells. Cold, damp wind. Daylight is bright and hurts our eyes.

The men lead us through the ship. Mother can't climb the metal ladders, so they lift her, but I won't let them touch me. I push them away. Climb on my own. Greasy rungs slip through my hands. I fall once. Twice. Scrape my shins. I'm shaking from the cold and the fright and the hunger in my belly.

It's cold in the building they bring us to. That and all the white people are enough for me to know we're far from home. I hope it's somewhere safe. I want to drink the hot tea they give us, but Mother won't let me. She hides behind me. The men ask lots of questions and I am certain now they're speaking English. Neither of us speaks. A man with a first-aid kit arrives. Mother turns her back.

'He's a doctor,' I say. It makes no difference to her.

He bandages my bleeding shins. Checks my eyes, ears, mouth. Listens to my heart.

'Where is this?' I ask him.

'You're in Ireland now.' He smiles. He speaks English slowly.

'We want to apply for international protection,' I say. I've practised this over and over since leaving home. 'Please help.'

'I'll tell them outside. You must make a formal application in a few days – don't forget.'

After he leaves, they bring us sandwiches in a packet and water. We're exhausted and tired and hungry. The sun is dropping when there's a knock on the door. A bearded man comes in. He says nothing, but leaves two coats on the table, smiling. Working men's coats, smelling of oil and hard labour. Warm and comforting. We wrap them around us. Curl up on the floor. Mother sleeps for a while. I watch the moon rise over black water.

A man in uniform arrives. 'We've a room sorted.'

I stare out the car windows at trees bending in the wind. The ground is littered with pale leaves shining in the car lights. Shrubs and hedges are wind-twisted. I shiver inside the big man's coat.

'This is their summer,' I whisper to Mother.

'Imagine how their winter will be,' she says.

.   .   .

I hardly remember the first few days. I'm tired and scared and cold. Everything is strange and confusing. Other women sleep in a large room with us, but we don't speak to them. We sleep a lot. Eat little. Talk less. We curl up together in the same bed, holding each other. We go downstairs for food on some days, but I hardly recognise what's on our plates and am usually sick after. They give us spare clothes. Towels. Soap. It's four days before I remember the doctor's words about a formal application. I ask one of the other women about it.

'Is it too late? Will we be sent home?'

'Go to the government office – the IPO,' she tells me. 'It's the International Protection Office in the city. Someone goes from here almost every day. You'll have company.'

They give us bus money at the front desk. It's wet and cold when we leave the Centre with three other people. We arrive before the office even opens but there's already a queue.

'So many people looking for this protection,' Mother says.

White people in suits and smart clothes stare at us as they walk past. When the office opens, we're given a ticket and wait all morning as they call out ticket numbers. The waiting area quickly fills up with people. They're talking many different languages. It's noisy and busy. Crying children and babies.

Our turn comes at last and we're called into a small room with a desk. My heart sinks when I see a man is about to interview us. This is not good. What man is going to believe a woman? Government officials don't listen to women.

'This won't go well,' I whisper to Mother.

'Do whatever he tells you,' she says. 'He knows best.'

I glare at her. She always believes that men know best. That they should be in charge. She doesn't question if it's fair or right.

The man speaks slowly and asks simple questions I understand. I translate for Mother, but she shakes her head and refuses to answer. She won't speak in front of this unknown man when we have no male relative with us. At home, Father dealt with all official matters. Mother never went to school. She can't read or write, and as a woman, was never allowed to speak up. And now that she needs to, she won't.

'You need to answer my questions,' the man says. 'I can't help if you won't speak to me.'

When I translate his words, Mother turns her back and says nothing.

The man makes a phone call. Turns on a speaker, and a woman speaks our language to Mother and me, and English to him. This is good for two reasons: first, she's a woman; second, we understand her. I take a deep breath and pray that Mother will answer now, but it makes no difference: Mother won't speak to any of us.

'I can answer instead,' I tell the man. My stomach twists even as I say this. What if I say the wrong thing? What if I get us sent back home? I left school at twelve, so my English isn't good. I can't put words on the feelings waking me at night. Mother has a different memory of what happened. If she would speak up, she could tell our story.

'That's not allowed,' says the man. He sounds annoyed. 'Your mother is the adult. She must respond.'

'Please, Mother,' I say. 'Just answer the questions.'

But Mother won't even look at me. The silence in the little room stretches out. I'm hot and uncomfortable. Finally, the official pushes back his chair and stands up.

'This is most irregular,' he says. 'I need to talk to someone.'

He leaves the room as the woman interprets his words.

'This is not normally permitted,' the man says to me when he comes back. 'But on this occasion, we'll allow you to respond instead of your mother. Are you OK with that?'

My stomach flips as I nod and try to settle down.

And the questions come like monsoon rain:

- Where are you from?
- Why are you here?

- How did you get here?
- Why can't you go home?
- Where were you before you arrived here?
- Why do you want international protection?
- Why did you leave your country?

I don't know what to say. How to answer. The man talks to the interpreter. She tells me to relax. That it's OK. To take my time. He smiles. I take a deep breath and begin.

Explaining why we left our own country, and what happened to us is the hardest part. All that remembering. All that reliving. For weeks, I've been trying to put it out of my head. Trying not to remember. But now, I awaken all the terrible memories crouching inside me. Things I'm scared to remember, scared to forget. I put words to the memories for the woman on the phone and the man who doesn't understand me. The remembering brings powerful feelings with it, feelings that cut my heart open until my voice shrinks small. I can't get the words out. Can't make myself understood through my sobs and tears.

The man types into his computer, watching my face as I describe our last days at home. How we had to run for our lives. He gives me a break. Brings me a glass of water. Mother squeezes my hand.

As the questions go on, I think Mother's ghosts have fled her tormented thoughts and come to live in my head instead: Sharnaz's voice. My father's. Uncle Rashid. I smell the mango tree and water lilies. Feel the hot sun on my skin. When I finally reach the end and tell them about the men finding us on the ship, my energy is gone. I drop my head. Draw breath. I have nothing more to tell.

But it's not yet over. The man prints out pages and pages of typing. My story. He reads it back to me, word for word. Slowly. Piece by piece, the woman translates it for me. I live my story yet again through their words. Mother sighs and shakes her head. I listen like my brothers listened to my made-up stories at home. I don't own it any more. It's my story, but I've given it away. In some strange way, that's a comfort. It's now on paper for someone else to read. The man hands me a pen and I write my name at the end of my story, our story, to show it's the truth. He keeps a copy and gives me a copy for myself. A book of what happened to us. Then, we're photographed and fingerprinted.

By the time we're finished, I'm exhausted and shaking and cold. We wait outside in the rain until the others are finished and travel back to the Centre together. I don't cry until we get to the room we share with the other women. They gather around, murmuring and bleating like goats fretting for their kids.

'It's so hard,' they say. 'Such a difficult thing, this first interview.'

'Why photographs? Fingerprints?' I say. 'What have we done?'

'It's for everyone,' they say in English. 'Doesn't mean anything.'

'At home, they only photograph and fingerprint criminals.'

'It's part of your application.' The women smile and rub my back. 'Now you must wait for their decision. That's the hard part.'

The next day, my tiredness and fear take over. I feel ill.

'It's sadness coming out,' Mother tells me. 'No longer deep in your heart.'

'What if they don't believe me?' I ask. 'What if they decide it's not true? That we're dishonourable women? What if they decide to send us back to our village, back to Father?'

I lie in bed all day, but my heart won't let me rest. My thoughts run wild. My head is haunted with memories. In my waking nightmares, the Irish office sends our photographs and fingerprints to the village council and we're found. Every plane passing overhead carries Father and Uncle Rashid to drag us home.

Days pass slowly.

The women in our room get their official letters and move on. Others arrive to fill their beds, tired and upset and usually cold. We tell them about the bus to the office in the city. Comfort them when they return from their interviews.

'This place is filled with sadness and suffering,' Mother says. 'The walls only hear stories of loss and heartache. Of the graveyards in our hearts.'

.　　.　　.

Our letter finally arrives to say we can stay in Ireland to finish our application.

'Are we safe now?' Mother says. 'Can we live here?'

'Not yet,' I tell her. 'This is the beginning.'

'You're moving on now,' the man in charge tells us. 'Can't stay here once you've got your letter.'

'Where to?' I ask.

'No idea,' he says. 'You're in Direct Provision from here on.'

I don't know what this Direct Provision means. I don't know that it will become our life. He gives us money for our journey and, written on a piece of paper, the address we must go to and the buses to take us there. I don't sleep on our last night. I'm too scared of where we're going next. Mother and I on our own, finding our way across this new country.

We leave early next morning and arrive later that day at a dark old house. They give us bed sheets and toilet paper. Bunk beds in a room with four other women, none from our home country. No planes overhead. A toilet and wash-hand basin between us all. Shower room down the hall.

Mother and I sleep together in one bunk, wrapped around each other. We leave the top bunk empty. Every morning, I wake in the darkness to stare out the window at cold fields. Watch grey daylight creep into the night sky. The room is always chilly. Condensation drips down the glass. One of the panes is broken. When I touch it with my fingertips, cold air scrapes like a blade over my skin. It reminds me of a broken window in our home, a long time ago.

We don't talk to the other women. They move around us, rustling, rummaging, talking, in another world, as though a veil separates them from us. Mother spends her days curled in bed, staring at the walls. The pillow is damp from her tears. She has little to say. She sighs and rubs her shoulders and legs as though her bones hurt. She complains of the weather, the food, the people, the light. She doesn't like the window open because she gets cold. She doesn't want to get up or to eat. When I hug her, her bones are sharp and hard under her skin.

They give us money every week. Mother and I look at the coins and notes.

'What's it worth?' Mother asks.

'I don't know.'

I recognise the coins from the bus money we were given but don't know their value. Father looked after the money at home. Irish money means nothing to me.

. . .

Time passes. I don't keep track of the days. It's always dark now. Always cold. Just when it seems the sun will never rise again, I begin to wake up. Come out of my dream world. Little by little, I notice things. Recognise the women in my room. Before, I didn't know any of their faces but now I know them all. The white woman on her own lies on her bed, rocking and picking wallpaper from the wall, peeling it off in long strips. Two older brown women seem to speak a little of the same language and talk to each other, although they're strangers, but I can tell from their hand gestures and the way they stop and start that it's not their native language. The black woman is with two young men in another room. Across the hall is a men's room. A tall man with brown skin and heavy brows watches me. He wears white *shalwar kameez*. Leather sandals. Black socks. I've never heard him speak so I don't know his language. Always on the landing when I pass, his dark eyes linger on me. I know how men watch women. That look they have. He frightens me.

'He watches me all the time,' I tell Mother.

'Do you think he knows your father?' That's all she's worried about.

I shake my head, reassuring her. 'It's how he watches me. How he's always there.'

'Don't go out on your own,' Mother says. 'Only with me or the other women.'

We come and go in twos and threes and there's comfort and safety in it. It feels familiar. It's what women do at home. The other women smile and nod at us. They welcome us with them. Tell us what happens next.

'Only legal people know how to fill in the forms,' they tell me in English. 'People with special schooling. Don't send anything in without their help.' They give us addresses for legal aid. Phone numbers. 'Ring them,' they say. 'Tell them you need their help. Show them your story.'

When I ring the legal aid people, they tell me to contact them after the government office has written. They send more information to read, more forms to fill out. I put them with my typed story.

The government papers arrive soon after: a thick packet filled with official documents. So much paperwork scares me. I left school almost three years ago. How do we do this? I pull out the papers the legal people sent me. Try to figure out what I need to do. Mother is no help.

'Go and see them,' the black woman tells me. 'Meet them and talk to them. It's easier.'

It means we have to find out about more buses. More places to find. More travelling. Mother doesn't want to come with me. The heartbreak of home fills her heart and soul and stops her doing anything.

'I'm tired, Azari,' she says.

'We have to get this sorted, Mother.'

'You go. I need to sleep.'

'We need to do this today. They're expecting us.'

'Then you go ahead. I'll be here when you get back.'

I can't do this alone. I'm too scared. 'Please, Mother.'

'We'll go tomorrow,' she says, closing her eyes. While she sleeps, I ring the legal aid people. Ask to meet them the next day.

We spend the whole day on buses and in offices, listening and talking and signing forms. We meet a woman called Sheila who agrees to help us. She insists on speaking with Mother, not me.

'You're only a child,' she tells me. 'You're not allowed do this. It's not legal. I have to speak with a responsible adult who understands what's happening.'

'My identity card says I'm eighteen.' I hand over the card Father got me when I left school.

Sheila looks at the card. She turns it over. Looks at me.

'This is fake,' she says. 'You're a child.'

She calls an interpreter but this time it's a man: Mother refuses to speak to him. Sheila prints out information in our language to show her instead, but Mother pushes it away. Turns her back.

'She can't read,' I say.

In the end, Sheila talks to me about everything, even though I'm only a child. She shakes her head. 'I shouldn't be doing this.'

She runs through the same questions the man in the IPO asked. It's not so difficult this time around: she's a woman and I already have my written story to show her so I don't have to relive it. She's not happy I was interviewed alone in the IPO.

'I wasn't alone,' I tell her. 'Mother was there.'

'It's obvious you're a child. You had no legal representation. And your mother …' She looks at Mother, scowling and refusing to speak. 'This is not good.' She pauses for a moment, then appears to make a decision. 'Fine. I'll meet you a few times to make sure we get our information right and have everything we need.'

She makes an appointment to meet us the following week and we return to the Centre. I'm ready for the sadness to come out this time, for the tiredness to hit me. I rest the next day. Let my tears come as they wish.

.   .   .

Weeks stretch out. It rains for days on end. The orange and gold leaves are gone. Only bare trees now.

We meet Sheila three, four, five times. I sign papers, answer questions, listen to the interpreter. Whenever there's an appointment, Mother refuses to come with me until I plead with her.

Every time, she asks if the decision has been made. Every time, I tell her we're only at the beginning.

My head aches. There's nothing to do in the Centre but sleep.

'Come down to the television room,' the other women say.

We join them for a few nights. I like the music and colour on television, the exciting stories. It's like looking in on other people's lives. I learn things to say:

· *Where did you think you were going today – on a picnic?*
· *Say what you see!*

I hear strong words to call people: 'The Beast.' 'Dark Destroyer.' 'Vixen.' We don't stay long though because Mother gets a headache and feels tired. At home, she was busy all the time, from dawn to dark, and never seemed to be as exhausted as she is now. I'm not tired. I need to do something. To get out of the Centre for a while.

'We can't go out,' Mother says.

'Why not?'

'It's not safe.'

'We've been on buses lots of times.'

'I'm not well, Azari. Stay with me.'

What happened back home shreds my sleep. I lie in the dark, reliving everything. My legs and arms twitch. I need to break the tedium or I'll go crazy. Need to do something. If Mother won't get the bus somewhere with me, I'll have to stay close to the Centre.

'I'll go for a walk,' I say.

'On your own?' Mother says.

'I've seen women walking on their own here, Mother. It's safe. It's allowed.' I look at her as an exciting idea pops into my head. 'I might even *run*!'

Even saying the word gives me a little zip of excitement. Father stopped me running: *Women don't run, Azari.*

'You can't,' Mother says. 'Your father told you not to.'

I look at Mother. I take a deep breath. 'Father's not here, Mother. He can't tell me what to do.'

She shakes her head. 'Women don't run. You know this. Your father told you.'

'Perhaps Father was wrong.' I'm treading a dangerous line.

'Men are never wrong, Azari.' Mother sets her mouth in a tight line. 'Your father was not wrong. He knows these things.'

Now is not the time to argue with Mother. I need to do something for myself.

The girl on the front desk is not much older than me. She might be a good person to ask. It takes me days to work up the courage to speak to her.

I stop at the desk. She looks up from her phone.

'Can women run here?' I ask.

'Do you mean like jogging?'

'Is that running?'

She nods. 'It's fine to run, but not after dark. Otherwise, you're grand to head out. Are you a big runner?'

I'm confused. 'This size.'

She laughs. 'I mean do you run a lot?'

'Not for a long time.' The girl is nice. 'And for running clothes?'

'You'll get runners and leggings in the department store in the main shopping centre.' She points out the door. 'About half an hour. Out the gate, turn left.'

Next morning, I'm up and dressed early to walk to the shops to get running clothes. Even though she's not happy about it, Mother gives me money.

'Come with me,' I say. 'We'll be together. We'll mind each other.'

She refuses. The other women are more encouraging.

'You'll be fine, girl,' they say. 'It's safe to walk alone here.'

'I'll watch you from the window,' Mother says. 'And I'll wait up until you get back.'

'It's a short walk. I'll be home by lunchtime.'

The whole way to the shops, I'm terrified. Women don't walk alone at home. I pretend I'm with Sharnaz, walking like we used to in our village. I hold a whole conversation with her. I've been talking to her more and more lately, and she chats back. It brings her closer. I imagine she's here.

Pull yourself together and stop being such a chicken, Sharnaz says. *We got the bus into town together and it wasn't a problem for you.*

'I know,' I argue. 'But you were with me. I knew where I was going. How to get home. I knew the village, the town, the route. Every one of those things is different now.'

You've come from our little village all the way to Ireland and you're still alive. You've been on buses around Ireland. This is only something small. I'm with you. We can find out together.

It's early afternoon when I get back to the Centre. My anxiety has tired me out but I'm proud of myself. Mother is fretting in the room.

'I thought you'd never come back,' she says. 'You said you'd be back by lunchtime.'

'It took longer than I thought,' I say. 'I got extra things we need.'

I tip my shopping onto the bed. Mother studies the women's undergarments with interest. She unrolls the socks, unlaces the shoes. Checks the stitching on the warm sweatshirt. She comments on it all. It's the most interested I've seen her since we arrived. She looks at the leggings and running shorts.

'You shouldn't be running around in tight clothes for everyone to look at your body,' she says.

I try on my new running shoes. They're not as supportive or flexible as my shoes at home, but they're fine. I'm excited about the idea of running again.

That afternoon, Mother washes herself in the bathroom with a basin of warm water. I try the shower. First, I pick a thick clump of hair from the plughole. Peel apart the grungy shower curtain. Test the temperature of the water. It's not hot for a very cold country.

Afterwards, we put on clean warm clothes. I comb out Mother's hair until it is gleaming and straight. She plaits mine and pins it up. The other women smile at us and nod. The younger woman gives us hair clips. We wash our old clothes and hang them on the heater to dry. Being busy and sorting ourselves makes me feel better. Mother too is a little brighter in herself. I make sure we're both downstairs early for dinner. For the first time, Mother almost eats a full meal. As we're leaving the canteen, the same girl is on the front desk.

'Last night here for you,' she says. 'You're moving tomorrow.'

I stare at her.

She points. 'It's on the notice board.'

I hurry over but can't get close enough to see. A dozen or so people peer at lists pinned on the board. While I'm waiting, I fret about how this might affect our applications and documents and legal aid. How will I contact Sheila if we're leaving tomorrow? How will I manage to meet her to sign documents and answer questions?

When I get to the notice board, the lists are difficult to figure out. I keep forgetting to read from left to right.

Mother fusses beside me. 'What does it say? Are they sending us home?'

Tracing down with my finger, I find our names halfway down the second page, the name of the Centre at the top. A woman with a baby stands beside me. She glances at where I'm pointing. 'You're going there? It's the middle of nowhere. You'll be left for months – forgotten about.'

'In Ireland?' I ask her.

'Sure is, but not anywhere you'll want to go.' She pulls a face as though she's sorry for me, then walks away.

'What did she say?' Mother asks.

'We're going to a safe place,' I tell her. 'Where Father and Uncle Rashid will never find us.'

Chapter 2

When I was seven years old and Sharnaz was nine, the famous runner Jinani Azad won gold for my country in the summer Olympic Games. She broke the world record for women in the 5000 metres. Mother had tears in her eyes when she told us.

In celebration of her victory, the government announced a national holiday. Jinani came from my province so everyone in my village went wild with excitement. Celebrations lasted a week. We had bonfires and fireworks, dancing and singing. Kashif and Musa were toddlers, so we put them to bed as usual, but Father allowed Sharnaz and me to stay up late to watch the village celebrations.

It was something special.

Musicians played traditional songs of celebration. Men and women danced and sang in the street, happiness filling the night air. Sparks and flames spun high in the night. Women tore apart roast goat meat to share around.

Late that night, Mother pulled me and Sharnaz close to her. She looked around to see where Father was before she whispered in our ears.

'Listen, girls.' Her voice was hoarse from smoke and laughter and singing. I stared at the firelight dancing in her dark eyes. 'Women are not as important as men. Men can do so much more. That's the way it is. But today is something special for women. Today means sometimes women *can* be important! When you grow up, look back and remember tonight.'

Even at that age, I knew she was telling us something special. In my heart, I wanted to be the next Jinani Azad. I wanted my village to celebrate my achievements as a famous woman.

When we went back to school, our teacher told us a new running club for girls was being set up in the village. There was already a cricket team in the boys' school, but nothing for girls. The village council wanted more women athletes from our province like Jinani to win gold medals in the Olympics. Father was on the village council and agreed Sharnaz and I could take part. My cousin Iman and our friends Ruba and Deeba joined too, along with most of the girls in my school.

We loved attending after school. Instead of walking straight home through the fields to attend to our chores, we raced and jumped on the dirt road in front of the school. Our teacher organised little races between us. We played catching games with small balls.

Deeba and some girls stopped attending after a few weeks, but Iman, Ruba, Sharnaz and I stayed on, enjoying the exercise and the freedom. On running days, we were excused from working in the fields because the club was supported by the village council. We still had to do household chores when we got home, but even so, we counted ourselves lucky.

As the weeks and months went by, we got stronger and fitter. Instead of dropping the balls, we learned to catch them. Instead of flinging them wildly, we aimed more or less accurately. We raced each other home along country lanes and across the fields, laughing and panting when we arrived.

A year or so after the club started, the village council approved money for our teacher's husband to do a training course and he became our coach. Our teacher supervised as Coach developed our games and activities into something more organised. We still had fun, but now we were split into teams and age-groups: under-tens, under-nines, under-eights. We jumped over sticks propped up on rocks. We ran team relays with balls. We balanced on wobbling planks. Our club got bigger and better as girls from neighbouring villages joined up. We met twice a week. Started running at weekends.

One day, Teacher and Coach walked us to the girls' school an hour across the fields to another village where we competed against the girls' school there, running races and relays along the street while the teachers held string across the road for the winners to break through. I won nearly all the races I ran. I got known as a fast runner.

The most exciting news came when Coach was awarded a grant from an international sports company to buy running shoes for us: thirty pairs in five different sizes. It made everything real when boxes of brand-new running shoes arrived in a delivery truck to our village. We opened the boxes in the school room, laughing with excitement.

'They're so clean and shiny!' Sharnaz said.

Iman pulled a new pair out of the box. 'White laces!'

'Will these make us run faster, Coach?' I wanted to know.

Coach measured our feet and handed us each a pair of shoes. It felt strange at first wearing tight laced-up shoes. We stomped around the class and laughed at each other with our big clean white shoes. They felt heavy, but Coach said they would improve our running no end.

'They'll be so much better for your feet than running in your own shoes,' Coach said.

'Better than barefoot?' Ruba asked.

'Much better,' Coach said. 'We'll keep them in school.'

'We can't bring them home?' I asked.

'What's going to happen as soon as these shoes go home with you?' Teacher asked. 'Your brothers will take them for cricket. Your fathers will give them to your brothers. Your cousins will borrow them for *their* brothers. They'll get lost. Damaged. Taken. You'll never get to wear them.'

She was right. We nodded in agreement.

'They'll be here for safe-keeping. For the running club only,' Coach said.

At first, nobody wanted to wear the running shoes on the dirt road in case they got marked.

'Don't be foolish,' Coach said. 'Run! Run! Go on. Off with you!'

Once we got used to them and our blisters healed up, the proper shoes gave the running club a whole new life. We felt professional and serious. I loved it all and trained hard every week. I started running everywhere I could.

'I'll bring those green mangoes to Aunt Hania,' I'd offer Mother, wrapping them up in a cloth. Away I'd go, running as fast as I could. Aunt Hania is Mother's sister, Iman's mother. They live half an hour's walk from the village but if I ran, I could be there in half the time. I ran to and from school instead of walking. No matter how I pestered her, Sharnaz wouldn't run with me.

'You're lazy!' I'd tell her. 'You want to gossip with Ruba.'

'I spend my evenings running after Musa and Kashif,' Sharnaz said. 'That's enough for anyone.'

Two years' older than me, Ruba and Sharnaz talked about boring stuff – marriage and boys and school. In the morning when they walked to school, I was happy to leave later and run to school instead. I challenged myself to see what time I could leave and still arrive in school before them. I enjoyed working my legs and pushing myself hard. Mother was happy about it because I was around to help her with chores before school. She told Father how much better it was for me to stay later at home, so he agreed I could run on my own across the fields.

In my club, I won all the races in my age-group. There was nobody my age in my village or the next who could beat me. I was nine by then and the best runner in the under-tens.

'I'm moving you up to under-elevens,' Coach said.

'Against Sharnaz?'

'You're well able for it.'

I was excited. Once I got used to the tougher competition, I began to win in the older age-group too.

'I run faster than Sharnaz,' I told my family at dinner.

'Why are you even surprised?' Sharnaz said. 'You're always running. You're like a little machine.'

'But you're taller than me,' I said to Sharnaz. 'And older.'

Sharnaz laughed. 'And you're stronger and faster.'

'It's not good to show too much pride,' Mother said.

'Don't neglect your chores,' Father said. 'You have responsibilities.'

'I still do all my work, Father,' I told him. 'I even do extra in the mornings before I leave for school.'

At the club, Coach told us how to improve our strength.

'Think of your chores as extra training,' he said. 'Don't neglect them or you'll anger your parents. Instead, build them into your routine.'

When I carried the brimming water buckets from the pump, I hurried as fast as I could to strengthen my leg muscles. When I was scrubbing clothes on the river stones, I balanced on one leg. I pushed myself hard.

The year I turned eleven, two things happened in our village. First, when the weather was still cold and the mornings were dark and frosty, Sharnaz left school. I was astonished.

'How come you're not staying until after the rains?' I asked.

Girls in our village always left school at the end of primary school. There was no secondary school in our village. Village boys sometimes got the bus to the secondary school in town, but never the girls. Some, like Deeba, left even before the end of primary school to work in the kilns, but those were poor families with debts to pay off. I never thought Sharnaz would leave early. She always had her nose stuck in a book and wanted to go to secondary school. She had another six whole months ahead of her before she had to finish primary school.

'You won't have that bright future Teacher's always telling you about now,' I told her. 'It'll be all dark and miserable instead.'

We were cleaning the outhouse. It was a mucky job we never wanted to do – the flies, the stink, the filth. It was quicker if we did it together.

'Shut up, Azari,' Sharnaz said. 'You know nothing.'

'I know lots of things,' I said. 'For one, I know you're not going to secondary school now. And I also know you'll probably end up making bricks like Deeba.'

Sharnaz spun around, anger flashing in her eyes. 'It's not my choice! Father says I *have* to work.' She adjusted her scarf over her hair. 'For my future.'

Her words stopped me. 'Your marriage dowry?' I whispered.

'Girls are expensive,' Sharnaz said. 'With two of us at home, I have to start working.'

I swiped the air to scatter the biting flies. 'Where?'

Sharnaz turned away and started scrubbing again. 'One of the factories in town.'

'A *garment* factory? You said you'd rather *die* than work in those places – stitching from dawn to dusk. It's a prison.'

Sharnaz dunked her scrubbing brush in the bucket of water. 'Father got me a job through the council.'

We used to joke about slave labour in the garment factories. How everybody who worked there was indebted. Now my smart sister was going too.

'What choice have I? Join Deeba in the kilns and make bricks all day?' Sharnaz said. 'Anyway, sewing is a good skill to learn. It'll serve me well when I've a family.'

I scrubbed the wooden slats. 'I won't be working in any garment factory.'

'I'm leaving the running club too,' Sharnaz said.

'That's no surprise.' I sat back on my hunkers. 'You were never any good anyway.'

Sharnaz sloshed the rest of the water across the floor. She didn't even react to my teasing. I was annoyed now; she was no fun today.

'So, is that the rest of your life sorted then?' I said.

'What kind of stupid question is that?' Sharnaz swept the water away with the bundle of twigs. 'All I know is I'm leaving school, leaving the club and starting in the factory. That's it.'

'No need to bite my head off!' I grabbed the empty bucket and marched off in a huff.

.   .   .

The second thing that happened was near the end of the hot dry spring that same year. The Schools' Community Games were taking place in our provincial town, two hours from our village. A whole day of athletics in a real stadium. Nobody from our village had ever attended the games before but this year, Coach decided six of us were ready to take part. Mine was the first name he called out, then Iman, Ruba and three other girls in the club. We jumped and hugged each other and laughed with excitement. My stomach flipped at the thought of competing in a real stadium. I wanted nothing more than to share my news with Sharnaz.

Things had been different between us since she left school and started in the factory. I hardly saw her any more. She left in the morning when it was still dark, slipping out to catch the bus with the other women when the rest of us were only getting up. She often didn't get home until late at night after we had already eaten and the boys were in bed. She only wanted to wash, eat and go to bed, so we never got to talk and joke like we used to. On her days off, she was exhausted and wanted to sleep. Mother didn't even call on her to do any chores, so I was left with her work on top of my own.

Her mood was different too. She was distant and quiet. No interest in gossip from school or the club, no matter how juicy and fun I made it sound. We didn't laugh or chat like we used to. It was as though we had nothing in common any more. We were from different worlds and I didn't know how to bring her back into mine. I thought perhaps my exciting news about the games would be a way for us to get back to normal.

As soon as she got back from the factory that evening, my news popped out of me like bubbles. I could hardly get the words together, hopping and jumping beside her as she washed her face and hands.

Her reaction was nothing like I expected.

'What's the point?' she said. 'You'll be leaving the club soon anyway. Running in some old stadium makes no difference.'

I felt as though I'd been slapped in the face and didn't know what to say.

'Why would you even *say* that?' I finally managed. 'It's a big competition in a real stadium – that's huge! I'm not going to end up in a dead-end factory like you, Sharnaz. Just because you've wasted your life, don't think I'm going to do the same. I'm going to be a great runner like Jinani Azad.'

Sharnaz looked at me. 'When are you going to wake up and forget your dreams? They're never going to come true.'

Sharnaz had changed in a few months from my funny, smart sister to someone I didn't even recognise. 'I don't know why I bothered to tell you. You're like a sour, dried-out lemon. There's no point talking to you about anything!'

I turned and stomped away. I tried not to let Sharnaz's reaction ruin my excitement, but the fizz had gone out of me.

My cousin Iman arrived into school a few days later with exciting news: the garment factory where Aunt Hania worked was sponsoring running shirts for the six of us. We'd have team colours and proper running kit.

'We'll be like a real athletics' club.' I said.

'We *are* a real athletics' club,' Coach said.

After a great deal of discussion and arguing, we decided on blue and white shirts with the name of our village emblazoned across the front. They would look great. Even though I was so excited, I didn't tell Sharnaz. I figured she would be bitter and hurtful again and take from my happiness. But it felt wrong not to be sharing my excitement with her.

I missed talking with my sister so much.

As the games drew closer, Coach prepped us for the big day. 'It'll be noisy and crowded and busy in the stadium. You might be nervous and anxious. Be ready for it. It's normal. Focus on the track in front of you. Don't think about the crowds. You're strong runners. Great athletes. Run hard and fast.'

We whispered and laughed with excitement.

'You can bring two supporters on the day,' Coach said.

I asked Father that evening if Mother and Sharnaz could come with me. I had never been so far from home before and was nervous about travelling alone.

'Family duties don't get put on hold because of you,' Father said. 'Who'll clean and cook and mind the boys if they go? You'll be with Hania and Iman. Sharnaz has agreed to cover your chores.'

'Thank you, Father. Thank you, Sharnaz,' I muttered.

I was confused and surprised. Sharnaz had already spoken to Father and agreed to help out? I glanced gratefully at Sharnaz but she didn't look up.

Our running shirts arrived the day before the games, bright and shiny. I traced my finger over the letters of our village written on the front and couldn't stop smiling.

'Go to bed early tonight,' Coach warned us. 'Get proper rest.'

The next morning, the minibus collected us early: six athletes, Coach and Teacher, two mothers, a couple of brothers and sisters, and Ruba's father, who was our driver. The other mothers brought treats to eat but Coach was strict.

'No sweets before the race,' he said. 'Drink water instead. You can eat what you like coming home.'

I squashed between Iman and Ruba. We chattered as the bus trundled through towns and villages. I missed talking to Sharnaz and sharing my excitement, and wished she was beside me so we could talk like always.

We stared in awe at the huge stadium when we arrived, enough parking for thousands of cars and buses. Inside, we looked at rows and rows of tiered seating, proper running tracks, crowds of people milling around.

'Where's the toilet, Teacher?' asked Ruba before she threw up with fright.

While we got settled, Coach went off to find out about our events. The morning was for younger athletes. We watched the little runners line up at the start line to run their short races. Medals were handed out straight after the race, the winners lifted onto a podium for their awards. Schools left as they finished competing. By lunchtime, the stadium was emptier and quieter.

Coach gave us our race numbers and checked our shoes. We tried to look casual as we sized up the other runners, guessing who looked fast and strong. I imagined myself not in the stadium, but on an international podium, a gold medal around my neck, the national anthem playing for the whole world to hear. In celebration of my record-breaking victory, the government announced a national holiday. Everyone in my village – including my father – went wild with excitement. I was the champion of the world!

'Azari!' Teacher called. 'Come on. They've called your heats.'

I was up on my feet and running down the steps, through the gates onto the running track, Iman beside me. After hanging around all morning, it was happening fast. A race official checked our numbers on his clipboard, assigned us to our lanes. I was twitchy and anxious. I ran a short distance up and down my lane, working out the electricity in my legs, warming up. The running surface was springy and light, so my steps felt bouncy. I smiled at Iman, at the race officials clustered in the shade under sun umbrellas, up at the rest of our group.

It was time to line up on the starting blocks: six runners per heat.

The whistle blew and I was up and off, firing energy through my legs. The lane stretched ahead of me, curving around the stadium. I flew as fast as I could. The crowds were a blur as I raced past, hardly aware of the other runners. I saw the finishing line, officials holding the tape, and put on a burst of power, pushing myself hard. I was first across the line. I eased up, listening to the footfall and panting of the runners on my heels. Coach was there, and Iman too. We were hugging and laughing.

'Good time, both of you,' Coach said. 'Now take a break. You've both qualified.'

Ruba didn't qualify for her final, but she was still in the relay. One of the other girls fell in her heat and was disqualified. There were two other qualifications.

'Focus on your running,' Coach told us before our final. 'Stay in your lane. Don't mind anyone else.'

When my final was called, I got into position, hunched down, ready to go. I was nervous. The whistle blew and we were off, pounding down the track. My legs flew hard and fast. The springy surface propelled me forwards, bouncing me along. I was making headway, passing runners, but would it be enough to win? Iman was fast, but I overtook her, our blue and white running shirts blurring together. She gasped for breath, feet pounding the track. I drew closer to the lead runner as we rounded the final curve. There was nothing between us as we approached the straight, the tape stretched across the track in front of us. I put on an explosion of speed, lengthening my stride in a bid to get past. I saw the officials, the faces of the tape-holders. The crowd cheered.

We burst through the tape side-by-side and stormed across the line. I eased up and drew to a stop, bending over to catch my breath. The other runner slapped my back

'Great run,' she said. 'Not sure who made it.'

We shook hands and then I ran to find Iman and Coach.

'Fantastic run!' he said. 'Iman, definitely a new personal best. Azari, we might have a gold!'

I couldn't believe it. But we had to wait. The officials crowded together, reviewing the results, huddled over their papers and stopwatches. They finally came to a decision. The official walked towards where the runners clustered together. I was with Iman and Coach. He headed straight for me. I held my breath. But he kept walking. Passed me by. He gripped the wrist of the runner who had crossed the line beside me, lifted her arm high. Her team erupted with cheers.

'Silver!' said Coach. 'You won a silver medal, Azari.'

My heart was bursting with pride as I stood on the podium to receive my silver medal, heavy and shining, hanging on a silken ribbon. Our team and supporters cheered and shouted my name. It turned out the runner who had beaten me was almost a year older. I had run a new personal best, as did Iman and two of our other runners. And I wasn't the only medal winner that day: we won three bronze medals too. We sang and shouted and ate sweets all the way home, but deep in my heart, my joy was dampened because Sharnaz wasn't with me to share my memory. Because there would be no celebrations when I arrived home. But most of all, because I didn't win the gold medal.

Chapter 3

The bus leaves us outside town at a supermarket. A girl with a trolley of groceries and two small children points us towards the Direct Provision centre. She looks at us, bin-bags of clothes in our arms.

'It's a long way,' she says.

It takes us two hours to walk.

'My feet hurt,' Mother says. We stop several times to rest.

My stomach rumbles with hunger because we haven't eaten since breakfast. I'm worried we'll still be walking when it's dark, or that we've taken a wrong turn.

It's dusk when we trudge up a long driveway leading to a big building, four-storeys high, like a garment factory. Rusty staircases criss-cross from the top floors down solid grey walls. Clothes hang out half of the brown wooden windows, drying in the breeze.

A small knot of people are smoking at a wooden seat to

one side of the front door, watching us. The front hall is dim and smells of boiled food and damp clothes. We step past toys, baby buggies, odd shoes and three kids wrestling on the vinyl floor-covering. A woman upstairs shouts in a foreign language; the kids stop wrestling. Two of them race upstairs. A baby screams somewhere. Music blares from a room of sagging sofas and black teenagers who glare at us until someone slams the door.

'You missed lunch,' the manager says. 'Dinner's at six-thirty. You're on the first floor.'

He hands us each a book of rules, some towels, sheets, shampoo, toilet roll. We climb the stairs, squeezing past two men arguing. On the landing are toilets and showers. Down a side corridor is our room with one big bed. A stained mattress. A wardrobe with a broken door and three shelves. Black mould speckles the wall from the window sill, trailing down to the floor. Yellow net curtains in front of the window.

I sit on the bed. It creaks and sinks low. 'I think it's broken.'

Mother sits next to me. Kicks off her shoes. Her feet are swollen.

'Somewhere different every time, Azari,' she says. 'Is this our life now? No place to call home?'

·   ·   ·

A letter with an official stamp on the envelope arrives. Mother tenses as I tear it open, unfold the pages.

'Who is it from?' She hovers at my shoulder. 'What does it say?'

I look at the official heading on the page: Department of Education. I struggle to understand the formal language, searching for the meaning of unfamiliar words. I juggle the phrases in my head. Why is English so hard?

'You have to go to school,' I say.

'I'm not going to school!' Mother says. 'I never went to school. I'm an old woman. I'm not starting now.'

'No, wait.' I stare at the letter, figuring it out. My heart sinks as the meaning becomes clear. '*I* have to go to school.' I fling it aside. 'I'm not going to school. I finished school. I read and write. I speak English.'

'What would I do all day if you weren't here?' Mother says.

She gets back into bed for a nap, even though it's early. She spends most days in bed, sleeping her life away.

'You need to work,' I tell her.

She holds her hands out. 'These worked all my life. Now, nobody wants them. It has never been like this. I've never had nothing to do.' She looks at me. 'I ran the house. Cared for my husband. Reared children. For what? Nothing.'

'I want to work too. But they're sending me to school.'

'Such a waste,' Mother says. 'How will you run a household? Learn to cook proper food?'

Mother frets I'm not learning to cook or run a home. We haven't had proper food since leaving home. Real spicy food. Traditional dishes. The kitchen here is the same as in the other centres: not for residents. We get Irish food, same menu every week, in plastic cartons and paper cups.

All morning, I think about the letter. I've only met Irish officials: IPO staff, Sheila, the Centre manager. Now I'm starting school. I know nothing about school in Ireland. I know nothing about *nothing* in Ireland. I've stayed in three centres, been in lots of buses and one shop. That's all. That's not real. At home, I was always going places: other villages, the market, the town. I cooked and bought vegetables. Cleaned the house. Laughed with my friends. I walked with Sharnaz. Joked with my cousins. Played with my brothers. But here? All I know here are the centres and other foreign people we hardly speak to and the government officials dealing with our application. We're not part of Ireland. We're not real people at all.

'I need to get out,' I tell Mother. 'I can't sit here any longer.'

'Out where?'

'Anywhere. I need to do something. Stretch my legs. Fill my lungs.'

I grab my black leggings. Pull them on.

'You're not going out like that, Azari.'

I pull running shorts over the leggings. Lace up my new runners. The stitching at the heel digs in. They're not proper running shoes, but they'll do. I tie my hair back.

'I won't be long.'

Down the stairs and out the open door, I pause on the front steps, not sure what to do, where to go. It seemed like a good idea, but now I'm not as certain. Apart from the small knot of smokers chatting on the broken seat, the grounds look empty. I take a deep breath. Jog slowly over the gravel, moving my limbs. Easing into it. I circle the building, following a narrow path leading around the back. I get my bearings. Pass the windows of the kitchens, the canteen, the TV room. Some windows are open. Voices drift out. A radio or television. The smell of food frying. Sometimes, faces peer out at me. I pass a brown prefab, people queueing outside with bags of clothes. A row of low glasshouses, their shattered frames green with mould. A skip full to overflowing with used food cartons, black bin-bags, paper cups. My muscles flex and stretch, warming up, working. My runners pinch a bit at the back, but they'll ease out.

The day is cold and fresh but I'm already warm. The chill wind means nothing. After a couple of laps and some encouraging shouts from the smokers, I head down the driveway as far as the main gate. Stop at the cattle grid. A narrow track leads under old trees inside the walls. I follow it. It's slippery in places, muddy with dead leaves and puddles. I run past plastic bags snagged on bushes, coffee cups, dirty tissues. I slow down to keep my footing. Keep away from the brambles and thorny bushes. The trees open up to clear stretches where the sun is strong and bright. I find a tumbled-over swing set for kids, rusty under tall weeds and grass. A burst football. A broken bike. The track leads down a long valley, around fields of wheat and cabbages. They remind me of our own small field at home. Father grew corn and cabbages and onions. Tomatoes and beans. I'm distracted with thoughts of home.

After I trip over a clod of earth and nearly end up face down in the mud, I concentrate. Take it slowly, gradually build my speed. I push myself, drawing hard on my long-idle muscles.

They're stiff and unused to exercise. I push them harder. My heart pounds as blood pumps through me. I'm breathing heavily now, lungs working, drawing in the cold air until my chest aches. My life is hardly mine now, but this is something I can control. This feels good.

I enjoy it so much, I do another circuit when I get back to the cattle grid. My body's not as fit as it was, but how could it be? I've been doing nothing for weeks, months. I'm puffing and panting, my face burning, my lungs raw from sucking in cold air. I'm winded when I finish, but excited too. I went running!

I cool down as I walk up the driveway. My heart rate returns to normal. I'm happier than I've been for a long time. I enter the Centre, smiling to myself.

'Look at *you*, girlie, getting out in that fresh air and enjoying your *exercise*.'

I look up. A very dark-skinned woman stands half way up the staircase, a mass of black hair piled on top of her head. Six feet tall, a brilliant peacock in a pink dress with purple swirls. Headscarf of the same shade. And the biggest, sunniest smile you could imagine, big white teeth bright in her face. 'You must be a *serious* runner – I saw you *tear* past that front window like your feet were on *fire*!'

She leans on some words in a way I've not heard before. They jump out of her sentences and dance in front of me. She walks down the narrow stairs like she's on a stage in front of an audience, even though there's only me.

'I'm Princess,' she says. She towers over me. 'And who are you, little Nike.'

I'm shy with this woman's attention. I hardly speak to people other than Mother. I don't know what to say or what to do.

'Hey, don't be afraid,' Princess says. 'I've only *arrived* here, and I don't know *anybody* yet. All these new people making me *lonely* and scared and then you come *running* up to the front door like a goddess. Say hi to me. Make my ears happy. Make me a friend!'

She's funny and friendly. I've no idea why she's calling me Nike.

'You have a name?' she says.

'Azari,' I say.

'Azari. What a *beautiful* name! A name of the gods, but so much *sweeter* than Nike.' Princess says. 'You're a *serious* runner, Azari. Are you in training for something? Like, the *Olympics* or something?'

I laugh at the idea.

'Father stopped me running,' I say.

Princess looks around, as though expecting to see him. 'Is he here?'

'No – we left him behind.'

'So he's a long way away, Azari-Nike? Then you're *free* of his rules! Free to live your life and run like an *antelope*.'

'Mother's here.'

Princess bursts out laughing – a loud and rich sound that fills the whole hallway. Kids tumbling on the floor turn to look at her. Someone slams the door to the TV room.

'Do you always do what your mother and father want, Azari-Nike? Whose life is it anyway?'

• • •

I start school in January when days are at their shortest. It's different to school in my village. Classes here are long and hard. The school days stretch out until late afternoon and don't even end then. We get work-at-home in the evenings, which takes me hours.

From day one, I'm completely lost. I don't understand most of the lessons and anything I do understand is new and I'm way behind. I'm put in a class with girls two years younger than me. Even still, the gap seems wider every day. I get by with my spoken English, but the books are difficult. Words are spelt differently to how they're spoken, as though the language on paper sets out to trick me. I read and write our language, but it's not taught here. Instead, there are new subjects I never learned: geography, history, science, advanced maths. I spread my books on the bed at night, but usually end up with my tears dripping over them because I don't understand what I have to do. The information won't go into my stupid brain.

'Don't fret, Azari,' Mother says. 'You will be back working again soon and school will be behind you.'

But I do fret. Nobody in my class seems as stupid as me. I even sometimes wish Father was here to stop me going to school again; then I'm immediately guilty: Sharnaz would love nothing more than the opportunity I have to be at school.

The girls in my class remind me of my little brothers: giddy and bubbly and excitable. They're full of questions about my life back home. Why I came to Ireland. Why I'm older than them. Why I left my village. It's difficult to answer them all. I'm not ready to talk about Sharnaz and Father and Uncle Rashid. It was difficult to tell my story to the government official; I don't want to go over it again. I need to keep it close to my heart.

The school principal prepared me for their questions.

'The girls will be curious,' she said on my first morning. 'Don't share your history with everyone. Give yourself time to settle in. Find your place. Find friends you can trust.'

'English is my second language,' I tell them now. 'Learning in English is hard.'

'Are you staying in that Centre?' one girl asks.

'The one out the road?' says another.

'The place for foreigners?' In case I don't know where they mean.

They all wait for my answer.

I nod. 'The Direct Provision centre.'

It was a mistake to tell them. I know it as soon as the words are out of my mouth. Their faces change. They nod to each other: *told you so*. It's as though they see me differently from then on. Something of their response rubs off on me. I feel ashamed. I don't want them to know where I live, but I can't undo their knowing.

These girls' lives are nothing like mine. They live in family homes with their brothers and sisters. Play camogie and foot-ball. Talk about make-up and clothes and music. Share funny videos, news and gossip on their phones. I can't talk about any of this stuff. I don't have a phone, and if I did, I wouldn't have anything to share. Or anyone to share it with.

My life is all about international protection and legal aid, plastic food in throwaway containers and fretting about my mother staying in bed all day. I share my evenings with dozens of strangers from dozens of countries who speak languages I've never heard. My nights are full of dark memories and haunting dreams.

The shame of where I live, along with feeling stupid and so far behind these younger girls, gets under my skin, itching me like sandfly bites. It's something I can't escape. It's something that makes me less than all these Irish girls, as though I have shameful secrets to hide, instead of being here because Mother and I had to run for our lives. The only way I can hide my shame is to disappear. To become nothing. Every day, I shrink a little more to a smaller, quieter Azari, until I melt away and am hardly visible, even when surrounded by people. In the middle of my class, in the middle of a school, in the middle of the town, it's possible to *not* be there. It's not what I want. It's not what I am, but when I'm not seen, the shame and the difference are less too. From when I arrive in the morning until I leave in the afternoon, I keep my mouth shut and my eyes down. The only time I talk is when a teacher asks me a question in class, but this happens less and less. I talk to Sharnaz in my head. Daydream about our village streets and my brothers. Hope Mother got up today.

This was never how I was before. In my village, I was the joker, always laughing and talking, always with my friends and my sister, always getting in trouble for my trickery. My father didn't like my outgoing nature.

'It's not good for a girl to draw so much attention to herself, Azari,' he told me. 'It gives the wrong message. Men and boys will have no respect for a garrulous woman. Show more modesty.'

My father wouldn't recognise me if he could see me now. He would think I have become my sister: a model daughter.

School runs extra classes for non-Irish girls to help us catch up. Eight of us from the Centre meet in the resource room every day. The Irish girls call it Black School. While the rest of my class are at Irish or French, we learn English and maths. The resource teacher assumes we're friends because we're all foreign, but nothing could be farther from the truth. We're from Asia, Africa, the Middle East. We hardly speak to each other. The brown girls don't talk to the black girls. The white girls don't talk to the brown girls or the black girls. The black girls only talk to each other. Everyone is different. We're from first year up to TY and sixth. Different languages and cultures and beliefs and experiences. We have only three things in common:

· English is our second language
· We live in the Centre
· We hate Black School

I hate that we're bunched all together as though we're the same. I don't want to be with these girls in the resource room every day for an hour. It sets us apart. Makes us stand out even more. There's no hiding when eight of us pour out of the room together.

'You shouldn't be here,' one Irish girl mutters under her breath as she pushes past us on the corridor one day as we're returning to class. I'm not even sure who she's speaking to.

'Me?' I ask.

'Not looking at anyone else, am I?' she says.

The girl with her joins in. 'She said you shouldn't be here. Sponging off tax-payers. My da says yous are only here for free handouts: jobs and houses and medical cards. Living for free and doing nothing.'

Her words are pointed. Angry. The darkness in her eyes makes my heart beat hard.

'Go back to Africa,' she says. 'You're not wanted here.'

'Go on back to your jungle,' says the first girl.

It's like they've slapped me in the face. I don't know what to say.

'Can't even speak English,' the first girl says. 'What did I tell you? No better than monkeys.'

'I speak English,' I finally say, my face burning. 'And I'm *not* from Africa.'

The school principal also prepared me for this. 'Tell me if there's any racist talk. I won't tolerate such behaviour in my school.'

But I tell her nothing. The same rules apply here too: don't tell or life will get harder. I keep my head down. Disappear even more.

Once a week we have PE. That's the best part of the week. Most of the girls moan about it.

'Do we have to go outside? It's freezing cold, Miss.'

'I'm after forgetting me runners. Can I skip PE this week?'

'Can we not learn rules of basketball in the classroom, Miss?'

But Miss Cullen ignores the complaining and herds us outside, even in the cold and rain. We jog around the sports pitches to warm up. Do sprints and relays. Basketball and camogie. Throwing, catching, stretching. I never played team games before but they're fun. I love the cold Irish air against my skin, the smell of damp grass, running around with a ball. It makes me want to do more, only harder and faster. I'm alive when I'm at PE.

'Great job, Azari,' Miss Cullen says. 'You've done sports before.'

'Only running.'

'Competitively?'

'A bit.'

'I coach runners after school twice a week. You should join us. We're always on the look-out for new members.'

'Really?' My heart jumps with excitement. 'Where, Miss?'

'She won't come, Miss,' shouts another girl. 'She's in that foreigners' centre out of town. They never go to anything.'

My heart sinks.

'This isn't your conversation, Maret,' Miss Cullen calls back. 'Two more laps of the hockey pitch.'

'Ah, Miss, I'm after doing four already,' shouts the girl.

'Hop to it!' Miss Cullen turns back to me. I see the change in her eyes: that flicker of sympathy. 'GAA grounds outside town on the Dublin Road. Twice a week, five thirty to seven. Come along next week. You'll love it.'

There are so many reasons I can't go:

1. The Centre is half an hour by bus outside town and the only bus leaves the town square at five; I'd have no way of getting back afterwards.
2. Dinner's at half six, no exceptions; I wouldn't get an evening meal.
3. I don't even know where the GAA grounds are, how to get there, or how to get back after.
4. Legal aid people ring in the evenings most weeks to review forms and papers and go through our application; I can't miss the calls and Mother can't take them.
5. My work-at-home takes the whole evening.
6. How would Mother manage if I was gone two evenings a week? She just about manages with me at school all day.
7. We don't have spare money for extras. Things in Ireland are never for free. How would I pay?

'Maret is right, Miss,' I say. 'I can't go.'

'You sure? It's a great way to get to know girls your own age. A bit older than first years.'

'It's OK, Miss.'

Miss Cullen drops her voice so no-one can hear. 'We can make arrangements for you, if you like? Help you out.'

She's being kind. Trying to help. She feels sorry for me.

'It's OK, Miss,' I say again.

'If you change your mind, just let me know.'

'Thanks, Miss.'

I'm already away from her, running across the pitch so she can't see tears in my eyes. I can always run on my own, I think. Living in the Centre doesn't stop me. I have running clothes. Shoes. Running routes. And it's free.

Running is what it's about for me – not meeting Irish girls after school.

Chapter 4

The year after Sharnaz left school, our region went through a hot dry spell: not a drop of rain for months. The sun scorched the land. Crops in the fields shrivelled. The river dropped so low, foul-smelling green mud at the bottom dried out and cracked like broken pottery. Coach even stopped our training. Everyone prayed for the rains to relieve the dry.

Rats left the rubbish heaps and open latrines to run through the streets in search of water. My brothers chased them, along with the other village boys, yelling and flinging stones. A stray stone smashed the window in our house as a rowdy knot of boys charged through our yard after a rat. I came back from collecting eggs to find the boys staring at it, then they scattered.

When Father arrived home at dusk, hot and tired and hungry, the dowry curtains Mother had stitched by hand from her wedding dress were blowing through the shattered glass – faded peacocks and roses and jasmine fluttering in the evening breeze, dust from the yard already clinging to the fine silk.

Father shouted for me before anyone else.

'Azari.'

My heart jumped at his voice. I was inside, crouched on the floor, trying to piece together the splinters of glass, hoping against hope that the village repair-man could glue them together somehow, like he fixed almost everything the boys broke so Father never knew. It was too late this time. There was no sign of the boys of course. Father stood in the doorway, his shadow falling over me. My hands trembled so much the tiny shards of glass did their lethal work – slicing open my fingertips. Father saw the blood and decided I was the one who broke the glass.

'Get out!' he shouted.

I scrabbled into the corner, between the charpoy and the wooden shelves. As he lunged, I ducked away and was out the door before he caught me. He shouted as I fled into the field, where I crouched among the corn stalks until it was dark.

I crept home when the moon was high and dogs had stopped barking. The yard was silent, the door left unlocked for me. A dish of lentils and flatbread had been left out for me, covered with a bowl to keep animals away. I scooped water from the drinking pot. Crept into the house. The dowry curtains had been taken down. Pale moonlight shone through the broken window, painting the room silvery white. I waited at the door until I was certain Father was asleep: I'd known him to wait for me if I deserved a beating. That night, he was snoring. It was a good sign: he'd not likely go after me after a night's sleep. I climbed onto the charpoy next to Sharnaz.

'He knows it wasn't you.' Her whisper stirred the night air. 'Mother told him.'

The following week, the scorching weather broke. The rains came hard and heavy. The air shimmered with water and streets flooded with brown mud up to our knees. Water channels in the fields overflowed and washed away the shrivelled seedlings. Boys swam in the river and the pond, jumping and shrieking. It rained for weeks. We thought the clouds forgot to stop drenching the earth.

Between downpours, Father brought the boys into the field to plant seedlings. He taught them how to tend the corn and cabbages and tomatoes. They dug new drainage channels, pulled weeds, plucked weevils from the young plants.

In school, we were distracted by the heavy air. Teacher struggled to keep our attention as clouds rolled dark and low, charging the air with electricity and raising the hair on my arms.

One morning, weeks after the rains had started, my head ached more than usual. I had strange feelings in my stomach. Not sick feelings, but not normal either.

'What's wrong?' Iman asked when she saw me fidgeting.

'I don't feel right.'

'It's the rains,' she said. 'They ached Mother's bones all last night.'

Everything was put down to the rains.

When I went to the latrine at lunchtime and saw my undergarments, I got a shock. Something was wrong: I was about to die. I didn't say anything to Iman or my teacher. What could I tell them? Instead, I ran all the way home, splashing through mud puddles, frightened and confused.

Mother was preparing vegetables when I burst in, crying and breathless and mud-splattered. Sobbing, I told her what had happened.

'It's nothing to fret about,' she said. 'And you're not about to die. You're growing up, Azari, that's all. This is a special time for you.'

She took me out to the outhouse. Gave me a rag and told me to wash myself.

'You're a woman now,' Mother said when I came out. 'Keep this to yourself. It's not something to discuss openly, even with other girls.'

'A secret?'

'You're impure and unclean this week. It'll happen to you every month now until you're old.'

I stayed at home that week. Mother showed me how to look after myself and keep clean. She told me the many rules and rituals I had to follow.

'Never eat curd, tamarind or pickles while you are impure,' Mother said. 'Don't bathe in the river or cook food. Don't go alone through the village or people will think you have no morals or self-respect.'

'No cooking – how do women manage?'

'There are always other women around – sisters, friends, mothers. Women help other women, Azari,' Mother said. She tucked a strand of hair behind my ear. Smiled at me. 'You must behave like a woman now. Your childhood is over.'

I was confused and upset by this. It also didn't make sense. What had changed? But Mother didn't have answers, only warnings.

'Never again go into a field alone to relieve yourself. Always have another woman with you. Men could hurt you, Azari. Ruin your chances of getting married. Bring shame and dishonour on your family.'

I thought of Mother's words. How would I get to the running club if I couldn't be alone in the village or in the fields? Perhaps if Iman ran with me – but how would I tell her if this was a secret? How would men ruin my chances of marriage? When I asked Mother, she told me I would understand better as I got older.

While I was off school, Mother wouldn't let me do my usual chores. Instead, she sent me to the rubbish dump to collect metallics. For two days, I wandered among piles of scrap and rotting food, scouring for scrunched tinfoil, tin lids and drinks' cans. I spotted two of Deeba's little sisters scrabbling among the piles, no scarves on their heads, faces dark from the sun. They stared at me at first, but when I waved, they ran and hid among heaps of rubbish.

I washed my metallics at home and set them to dry in the sun, ready to sell. I scrubbed myself to rid my skin of the smell of the dump. Was I so unclean I could only be among rubbish and junk? I didn't want to be around my father or brothers. Didn't want to see my friends.

'Did this happen to Sharnaz?'

'It happens to every girl,' Mother said. 'Why do you think Sharnaz left school?'

I stared at Mother. 'Because of her marriage dowry?'

Mother shook her head. 'Nothing to do with that, Azari. Girls don't go to school after they become women.'

I hadn't known anything of this. Nobody told me – not even my sister.

'Deeba too – is that why she left?' I asked.

Mother shook her head. 'Deeba's family has debts. She left to work them off.'

A strange cold feeling settled through me. Would Father make me leave school also? And what of my running club? I was too afraid to ask Mother. If I didn't ask, perhaps the worst news in the world wouldn't come true. Father might not know about my being a woman because nobody was allowed to talk about it. I wasn't about to tell him.

Within a few days, my body returned to normal. All signs of being a woman were gone.

'Is it over?' I asked.

'Until next month,' Mother reminded me. 'We'll organise your cleansing now.'

A dozen women from the village gathered in our house for my cleansing. Mother and Sharnaz were present, but Father and the boys weren't allowed. The women rubbed my skin with almond milk and turmeric. They sang songs and made strange deep sounds in their throats. I felt special as the women sang for me. I had become part of a secret club only women knew about. They told me I was now ready for marriage, which made me feel sick and panicky. I had just turned twelve – marriage was the last thing on my mind. I was frightened by the changes this new thing was bringing to my life.

The night after my cleansing, I lay on the charpoy next to Sharnaz. 'Are you awake?'

'What do you want?' She didn't sound in the mood to talk.

'Why didn't you tell me?' I said.

'I thought you knew,' she whispered. 'Ruba and I were always talking about it.'

'I never heard.'

'You never *listened*. Most of the time, you were off running.'

'Did you have a cleansing?'

'Of course.'

'Where was I?'

'Running. Where else?' Sharnaz said. The words came out like she was spitting. 'It's all you ever do. All you ever think about.'

Her reply stung me. I was about to snap back, tell her my running was important because I was a good runner, but I stopped. My future might be different now. Father might stop everything. Sharnaz had changed from being fun and full of laughter to grumpy and snappy when she had had to leave school. She must've been miserable. I hadn't understood what she had been going through.

The news I dreaded came the next day.

'You'll start work now, Azari,' Father said at our evening meal. 'School is over.'

'What about running?' I said.

'Women don't run,' said Father.

'Jinani Azad runs,' I said in a small voice.

'Running is over.'

'I'm good at running, Father,' I said.

'It is over,' Father said.

'I could run after work.'

Father's slap was hard enough to knock me off my stool and tip my food to the floor. I never saw it coming.

Mother spoke up straight away. 'She means nothing by her foolish words, Nasir. She's new to womanhood. Forgive her.' And to me: 'Your father is right, Azari. No more running. No more school. It's finished now. Anyway, running makes your skin too dark. You look like someone from a poor family who works in the fields or the brick factory. No man wants to marry a woman who's too dark.'

I said nothing as I picked my rice off the floor. It killed me that my dreams of becoming an athlete were being taken away by being a woman.

Nobody spoke for the rest of the meal.

. . .

It was my last day at school, my last day at the club. I told my coach at training. He was almost as upset as I was, even though he'd heard the same thing many times before from his students.

'You've real talent,' he said. 'Does your father not realise how far you could go? You could get a place at a running academy with free secondary education. Perhaps even a college scholarship. Imagine the honour for your family.'

'Father says women can't run,' I said.

'What does your mother say?' Coach asked.

'That nobody will marry me if I'm too dark.'

'Marriage?' Coach said. 'You're *twelve*.'

Coach came to our home later that evening. We stayed in the house while he talked to Father in the yard. They shouted at each other. Father pushed Coach. Coach stormed out. I tore open the door and ran after him. Mother tried to grab me, but I was too fast. Out of the yard and down the street. I shouldn't be seen alone with a man, but I didn't care.

Coach turned when I called him, his face flushed, his eyes burning. 'Your father's not interested in you or your future.' I had never seen him so angry. 'He's only interested in himself. He doesn't understand that if you keep running, your whole family will benefit. I'm sorry, Azari. There's nothing to be done. Everyone's losing because of this.'

Sharnaz ran up to me as Coach stormed off. 'Mother sent me after you.'

She put her arm around my shoulders and I sobbed as my heart broke.

Even Mother tried to talk to Father. She told him how well I was doing with my running, that Coach said it would bring great honour and pride to my family and my village, that I could work in the day and train in the evenings. Father slapped and beat Mother around the house for challenging him. He insulted her and her whole family. Then he banished her to sleep outside for three nights for taking the side of another man against him.

I never went back to school. I never went back to my running club. Sharnaz and I were the best of friends again. She comforted me when I cried myself to sleep. She understood my heartbreak. For her, it had been school. For me, it was running. For both of us, it was every dream we ever had. And there was nothing we could do.

'You have to bury your dreams,' Sharnaz said. 'Father has the final say. That's how it is.'

My pain was fresher. Sharper. 'It hurts here, Sharnaz.' I pointed to my chest. I imagined myself living for ever with unbearable pain in my heart. 'I don't know how to live with the pain. Or without running.'

'The pain will never be gone, Azari, but you can trick your heart so the pain won't be so bad. Think only of today. Not tomorrow or next week or next year. Only today, you hear me? One day, your heart won't hurt so much. The knife won't twist so sharp. It's duller, like an old blade, but it will always be inside you.'

'That's not any comfort.'

'You've no choice, or it'll poison you from the inside. You'll end up making yourself sick.'

'Where did you learn this?'

'From Mother,' she said. 'It's what she did.'

I stared at Sharnaz. 'Did Father make Mother leave school too?'

'Sometimes you're even more stupid than you look. Of course, it wasn't Father, Azari. It was *Grandfather*. He never let

Mother go to school at all. She never got the chance we got. So count yourself lucky.'

'I don't feel lucky,' I said. 'I don't care about school. It's running I want. I was good, Sharnaz. I really was.'

'I know, little Azari.' Sharnaz hadn't called me 'little' in many years. It was her way of trying to soothe me. 'I know how you feel.'

And she really did.

.   .   .

As soon as Father collected my fake identity card stating I was over eighteen, I started work in the same garment factory as Sharnaz. We left the village in darkness to get the bus to town.

It was strange leaving home at such an early hour when the main street was quiet and empty. The bus was crowded with women heading to garment factories in town. They squashed up to make space for those of us waiting under the spreading tree outside our village. Sharnaz chatted to them as the bus trundled into town.

The sun was high when we walked out of the bus station, surrounded by bridges and highways and rushing traffic – more people and traffic than I'd ever seen. Cars, buses, cycle-rickshaws and trucks blasted horns and rushed along. Sharnaz grabbed my elbow.

'Move forward slowly,' she said. 'Don't stop. Don't step back.'

She pushed me onto the road and we moved slowly through the teeming traffic. As though we were wading through a fast-flowing river, the tide of cars, trucks, vans and buses parted. They moved around us. They didn't slow down. They didn't stop. They separated like a river flowing around a drifting leaf. We finally stepped onto the safety of the footpath on the far side. Turned down a narrow laneway to a tall grey building. Workers poured in the open door and we joined them, climbing a narrow concrete stair to a vast and crowded space three floors up.

I was nervous as I followed Sharnaz down the centre of the factory floor. All the windows were barred and screened. Nothing could be seen of the bright sunshine outside. Instead, the concrete ceiling was fitted with long electric lights and spinning fans. The fans flickered the harsh light and stirred snippets of thread and bits of fibre and dust through the sweating air. It was like everything took place behind a fine veil or mist. The thickened air caught in my throat. I coughed. Sharnaz scowled back at me.

'Shut *up*,' she said.

I scurried after her.

A racket filled the air so I could hardly hear my own thoughts. Scores of people operated noisy machines with hands and feet, feeding in lengths of cloth or cut-out shapes. Women reached and hauled heavy fabric, their dresses stained with sweat, their faces shiny. Men walked up and down rows of tables, pulling at garments, their voices raised, their words lost in the din. Piles of cloth and bolts of fabric were heaped on every possible surface: on the floor, on workbenches, in corners, in great wheeled trolleys, stacked against the wall.

Cardboard boxes piled high with garments stood next to almost every worker.

We passed one huge machine hissing and spitting and clanking. It shot jets of steam as a worker pulled a hot plate and lifted out smooth cloth. The rising steam added to the stifling heat which reeked of sweat and unwashed bodies.

At the end of the vast space, in the farthest corner from the door, half a dozen girls crowded around a wooden work-counter. Heads down, they worked silently through a stack of garments. Sharnaz introduced me to the man standing over them as her eighteen-year-old sister.

'Identity card?' he shouted above the din.

I handed him the fake identity card Father got me. He briefly looked at it, nodded and handed it back.

'I'll collect you at lunchtime,' Sharnaz said, and she was gone.

'Get to it!' the man said to me. 'Let's see if you're any good. Any slacking and you're out.'

One of the girls handed me a cutting tool. Another took a shirt from the pile and showed me loose threads at the collar, the cuffs, the buttons, the hem.

'Cut them off.' She snipped the threads tight to the fabric. She glanced behind at the man and then dropped her voice. 'He'll beat you if you damage the cloth or the buttons.'

'Who is he?'

'Jalal. Stay away from him.' She flashed a quick smile. 'You don't want to feel his fist.'

I started snipping but was slow compared to the others. They worked fast, flicking shirts over and back to snip threads before flinging finished garments into cardboard boxes behind each of them. I missed lots of threads to begin with. The girl who gave me the cutting tool kept a close eye on me – whipping the shirt from my hands and turning it over to show me threads I hadn't noticed.

'Here! And here!' she said. 'Put them in my box when you're finished.'

The girls chatted and talked as soon as Jalal moved away, falling silent and dropping their heads whenever he appeared close by. The heap of garments in front of us never got smaller. Every so often, a worker arrived with armfuls of new shirts. It was tedious, precise work and my legs ached from standing. I stretched my arms, my shoulders.

'Where's the toilet?' I asked the girl next to me.

'Back yard,' she whispered. 'Lunchtime only.'

Jalal appeared and pulled a handful of shirts from the box. He looked at each of them closely, flinging down the other girl's work. He thrust some of the shirts at me.

'Is this it?' He leaned down until he was in my face. His breath was foul. 'You need to work faster or you're out.'

My heart thumped in my chest even when he walked away. Jalal was a younger version of my father.

When lunchtime came, Sharnaz came to find me. We followed the girls and women pouring down the staircase to the back yard. Joined the long line waiting for the latrines.

'How's it going?' she asked.

I showed her my fingers, red and raw from hours of pulling and cutting threads.

'They'll toughen up.'

'Thanks for the sympathy.'

'Can you do the job?' she said.

'I'm slow. Jalal isn't happy.'

'Jalal is never happy.'

The latrines stank worse than the open latrines in the village rubbish heaps.

'No water in them,' Sharnaz explained. 'Drink less tomorrow.'

We squatted in the shade, joined by a girl from Sharnaz's section with a broken front tooth and a lopsided smile.

'Komal,' she said.

I smiled at her. 'Azari.'

We ate the eggs and flatbread we brought from home, our scarves draped loosely over our faces.

'A big order came in for overnight turnaround,' Komal said.

'Another late one,' said Sharnaz. She nodded at me. 'Lucky for you.'

'Why?' I asked.

'They'll need everyone they can get. Jalal will keep you on.'

My heart sank. Komal and Sharnaz laughed at my face.

'It's better, believe me,' Sharnaz said. 'Imagine Father if you lost your job on the first day?'

She was right: Jalal kept me on. I cut threads for another six hours until my fingertips bled and my shoulders ached.

'Eight o'clock in the morning,' Jalal shouted when we finally left.

It was pitch dark when we walked to the bus station. We hardly spoke on the bus. The village streets were dark and empty as we trudged home. I've never worked such a long day in my life.

. . .

I hated the factory. I hated what becoming a woman meant for me. I hated never seeing sunlight: dark when we left in the morning, dark when we came home at night. I longed for sunshine, the outdoors, the fresh air. I ached for my runs to and from school along leafy river paths, through sun-baked fields. The stretch and pull of my muscles. The freedom I never knew I had.

By the time I turned thirteen, I stopped noticing the flickering light, the sweating heat, the bad smells. My feet got used to standing all day. My fingertips were hard and calloused.

'Not noticing makes it worse,' I told Sharnaz on our way home. 'I *can't* get used to it. Then it's like I've accepted it. I'll *never* accept it. Don't you see?'

Sharnaz shrugged. She didn't see.

I dug her in the ribs. 'The pain in my heart is still here.'

'That takes longer,' she said. 'I already told you, only think of today. Not last year. Or next week. Or next month. Only today.'

'I. Can't.' I said. 'I want to run. I want to be outside. I want to be a girl again and not a stupid woman.'

She laughed. 'Show me you're not a stupid woman, Azari. Show me you can be my funny little sister.'

'She's gone,' I said. 'Buried too deep in my heart. She'll never appear again.'

'Do something for me,' Sharnaz said. 'Think of *one* positive thing about your work. Only one.'

I thought and thought. The bus rocked and lurched over potholes and through villages.

'Does it have to be big?' I asked.

'No, it can be something small.'

People got out. People got on.

'Does it have to be in the factory?' I asked.

'Yes. It must be about work.'

Still I thought. Finally, as we drew closer to our village, something came to me.

'I have it! I know something positive.'

'Really?' Sharnaz said.

'You don't believe me, do you?'

'Tell me your positive thing. Then I'll tell you if I believe you.'

'There's this broken window near where my work-counter is. It's up at the top where the metal caging ends.'

'And?'

'Every afternoon, for a little while, the sun shines through the tiny hole where the darkened glass is broken. It comes down in a bar of light. If I stand in exactly the right place – on the right side of the counter – it shines on my face. Just for me. My own special sunbeam. And when I get a face full of sunshine, I pretend I'm outside.' I smiled at Sharnaz. 'There! I thought of one good thing.'

'I believe you.' Sharnaz smiled at me.

We got off the bus and walked through the village towards home. The sun was low. Sweeps of orange and pink stretched across the sky.

'Why is Komal always so busy?' I asked Sharnaz.

Komal was smart and interesting. She watched everything going on, her eyes flickering around the women and girls. She always had information about what was happening in the factory: overnight orders coming in, a site inspection by European buyers, workplace accidents. Sometimes she left us to talk to other groups of workers as they ate lunch.

'She's the labour union leader,' Sharnaz said.

'What does that mean?'

'We've rights as workers,' Sharnaz said. 'We have to get paid properly. And treated fairly. Komal helps out if something happens to us. She talks to the supervisors and managers. And they have to tell her important news affecting the workers.'

'Will you ask her if we have the right to keep the money we earn?' I say. Every week, Sharnaz and I brought home our earnings and handed the money over to Father. He counted it carefully. Put it away. We didn't get any of it for ourselves.

'Sometimes I wonder if you have anything in your head.' Sharnaz laughed. 'Six of us at home to be fed and clothed. Two dowries. Father owes money on the house and land. He needs all our money, Azari. And you're looking to keep it? There's nothing you need. Father gives us food, shelter, clothing. What would you even buy?'

I thought for a bit. 'Maybe a mango lassi from the stand in the bus station.'

We turned in the gate to our yard.

The boys weren't playing cricket. No shouts of laughter or crack of the bat. Four men sat with Father on our best rugs, laid under the mango tree. Mother served them tea, fruit and sweets.

The men ceased their conversation as soon as we appeared. Sharnaz and I stopped our chatter. Pulled our headscarves over our faces, nodded to the visitors and retreated into the house. The men watched us but said nothing.

'What does Uncle Rashid want with Father?' I whispered once we were out of earshot. Father's brother lived in the next village with his family. We rarely saw them.

'And three from the village council?' Sharnaz said.

Mother came into the house behind us. 'Ghosts have been whispering in my head all week. I knew something was coming. Smelt it in the air this morning. I thought it was the Khan girl's breech birth, but the baby arrived safely last night.'

'Why are they here?' I asked. Father would never discuss business with Mother, but she might have overheard something.

'Something about a debt for a cow Rashid bought last year. He never paid the Sharifs. They complained to the council.'

'What does it have to do with Father?' I was indignant.

'Is it bad for me?' Sharnaz looked at Mother, her face stricken.

'You didn't buy a cow,' I said.

We stayed in the house with the doors and windows closed so the men's conversation was private. I kept looking at Sharnaz as though she might have answers. She looked worried. When it was fully dark, the boys crept through the yard and into the house. Mother sent them out with lanterns to set around the men.

It was late when Father finished his business and the men left. Sharnaz and I cleared the dishes, rolled up the rugs. The boys carried the lanterns inside. Father remained outside, the scent from his tobacco drifting in the window.

Mother settled the boys. They knew something was happening and were smart enough to keep quiet. There was none of their usual trick-acting and mischief.

'Go to sleep,' Mother told them. 'Or Father will be cross.'

'Go out and ask Father what his meeting was about, Sharnaz,' I said.

'And be beaten for insolence? Don't be stupid.' She looked at me sharply. 'You're not to ask him either.'

'Be quiet, both of you, and leave him in peace,' Mother said. 'He has had a long evening. Let him be.'

Then, Father called Mother out of the house.

Chapter 5

'Sheila got a letter from the IPO about our questionnaire,' I tell Mother.

'Questionnaire?'

We're in the concrete yard, queuing to get our turn using the washing machines in the brown prefab. There's always a queue for them: a straggle of people, bin-bags splitting with dirty clothes. Some leave their bags in the queue and go off for an hour or so, but we never do.

'It's very important,' I say. 'But Sheila doesn't think my English is good enough to fill it in over the phone.'

We shuffle forwards a few places. Set down our washing.

The prefab is one room: you open the door and you're inside. Enough space to squeeze past others with your bags of washing to get to the three washing machines – only two are working – and the dryer.

I glance at Mother. 'We'll have to travel up to meet her.'

'Not more travel? But your English is good enough, Azari,' Mother says. 'When I hear you speak to others, you have the words now. I hear the difference.'

Mother is right. It's easier for me to say things now. I understand most of what I hear, though I sometimes get stuck with tricky words, but not often. My English reading and writing aren't nearly as good: my spelling is terrible.

'I still have so much to learn,' I say. 'You've learned a few words here and there too.'

Mother smiles. She's picking up little phrases from TV shows she watches during the day. I've heard her repeat them to her new friends who recently arrived in the Centre. Mr and Mrs Farooq and their three children are from our home country. Mother and I get nervous when we hear others speaking our language, in case they know our region, our village, our family, but the Farooqs come from a different province. Even though they're Orthodox, it's good to have them here. They understand our ways and I'm so happy Mother has someone to talk to other than me. It's a good distraction for her.

'You'll manage the questionnaire with Sheila on the phone,' Mother says now.

That's her way of saying she doesn't want to travel by bus to meet her again. But it's not my decision.

'Sheila doesn't want to do it by phone. It'll take too long and we won't have the interpreter.'

'There must be someone locally,' Mother says. 'We don't have to go all that way. It's too far, just for a few papers.'

'I don't want to start over again with someone else,' I say. 'I like Sheila. She knows us.'

Two people come out of the prefab carrying clean clothes. We're next, except someone else's bag of washing is on the concrete in front of us.

'Should we wait and see if the owner comes back?' I ask Mother.

'They're not here,' Mother says. 'We're going in.'

She pushes the bin bag aside and marches in. I love when Mother is decisive and strong. It's good not to be the one making the decisions all the time.

Inside the prefab reminds me of our province during the rains: hot and humid. And it stinks as bad as the rubbish heaps in the village. Racks on the wall are supposed to be for hanging clothes, but the cables have rusted through and dangle down uselessly. Somebody twisted a couple of them around the window handle to make a clothes line, so the windows don't open. Black mould blooms across the ceiling like gathering clouds before a downpour.

I tip our clothes into the empty washing machine. Mother is adding powder and a token when the door slams open. A brown man with a furious face storms in.

'I was next in queue!' he shouts. 'You hopped over.'

Mother tucks herself behind me. 'What's he saying?' When I tell her, her eyes widen. She pushes me aside. 'I'm not a frog. You weren't here.'

As I translate for the man, Mother twists the knob to start the machine.

'You are the weakest link,' Mother snaps at him in English. 'Goodbye!'

I duck my head down so the man doesn't see me laughing. He's still standing there with his mouth open as we walk out of the prefab.

I toss and turn that night as I try to figure out what to do about our application. It's such a long way to get to Sheila. Two buses. A long walk each end. Mother finds it so difficult and tiring. But I don't think it's a good idea to start over with someone else. The IPO have already been in touch with Sheila and might not be happy with a new person. If only we could've stayed in the other centre until we had submitted our questionnaire.

I'm awake well before dawn and decide a run will clear my head. I slip out of bed in the darkness. Leaving a running sock on the pillow so Mother will know where I've gone, I'm out the door in ten minutes. The hall and staircase are quiet, only lit by the green of emergency exit signs. People talk behind bedroom doors. A baby cries. A shower runs.

The clock in the front hall says six thirty as I try to open the front door. It's locked and double bolted. I hear someone working in the kitchen and peek in the door. A man carries food boxes through open double doors at the back of the Centre.

'Get out!' he shouts when he sees me. 'Kitchen's out of bounds. Breakfast starts at seven.'

'I want to get outside,' I say.

'Seven o'clock,' he says. 'Come back then.'

'I can't get out now?'

He dumps a box on the counter. He looks irritated. Grumpy.

'I'm not supposed to let you, but … fine,' he says at last. 'Through this way. Just this once.'

I thank him. Slip through the kitchen and out the double doors.

'Seven from now on,' he calls after me. 'And only through the front door.'

The morning is fresh and cold. The dense black of night beyond the trees softens as dawn nudges into the sky. The days are getting longer. I run down the empty driveway. For the last few weeks, I've been exploring new running routes outside the grounds. I head out the gates, turn towards town and jog slowly, loosening my muscles, easing into the day. The countryside is waking up and I enjoy being part of it. Today it's dry and cold. Black hedges frosted with white. Once my limbs are loose and warm, I increase my pace, stretching into my stride, happy to be running.

By the time I get back to the Centre, the day is bright and a steady flow of traffic heads into town. My muscles zing from the run and my face is flushed and warm. Breakfast has started and I'm starving. Ever since I've gone back running, I can't seem to get enough food into me. I'm hungry all the time. I head straight in even before I've stretched: I don't want to miss breakfast and my packed lunch.

The canteen is full, the noise and racket rattling my head. I take a plastic-wrapped bowl of cornflakes and two slices of plastic-wrapped bread. Pour a paper cup of milk. They don't let you take more than one bowl of cereal and one plate of bread, but it's better than the other centre where they didn't serve breakfast at all. We got seven packets of pastries and seven apples on Monday mornings to last for the week.

Mother waves to me from the side of the canteen, a headscarf on the table in front of her. That'll be to make me a respectable girl. She's sitting with her new friends. As I walk over, the woman in the family takes in my clothing, her eyes sliding down my body to settle on my shorts and leggings. I sit, and Mother pushes the scarf across the table. I drape it around my head as she introduces me to Mr and Mrs Farooq and their three daughters.

Mrs Farooq ignores me. She frowns at Mother. 'You let her go out like that?'

The Orthodox Farooqs are more conservative than my family.

Mother manages to smile and look worried at the same time. 'Women runners dress like that.'

'Women and runners should never be in the same sentence,' says Mrs Farooq.

I spoon in cornflakes and think how she sounds like Father. Mrs Farooq turns to the older girl sitting beside her, who looks a couple of years younger than me.

'It is not right for girls to run, Fiza,' she says. 'Women should cover up and show modesty. Respectable women never run.'

Fiza stares at me, eyes round as saucers. I smile at her but say nothing. Beside me, Mother is picking at her bread – tearing it into little pieces – but not eating it.

'Are you going to eat that?' I whisper.

'What?'

'The confetti on your plate.'

She looks down. 'Do you want it?'

After demolishing her bread, I also eat her cornflakes and finally feel satisfied. I sign for my lunch sandwich and banana at the counter before running up to the room to wash and change before school.

'I didn't know where you were,' Mother says.

'Didn't you see my sock on the pillow?'

'That could mean anything! I don't want you running any more, Azari.' Mother packs my lunch into my schoolbag. 'Mrs Farooq says we shouldn't turn our backs on our customs because we're in a new country.'

I'm pulling on my school uniform, tying back my hair. 'I love being back running, Mother. It feels right.'

'It's not right. Nothing about women running is right. It's not proper to be seen in tight clothes. To be going out on your own looking like that.'

'You even asked Father to allow me to keep running, remember?'

'He was so angry about it,' Mother says, distracted by the memory. 'But he was right. Women should never be seen running. Especially in the dark. Especially on your own. Doesn't matter if you're in our village at home or here in Ireland. Mrs Farooq says Irish men will think you've no morals when they see you running and dressed like that.'

'It's none of Mrs Farooq's business,' I say.

Mother is quick to defend her. 'Mrs Farooq is one of our own. She knows our ways.'

'She knows nothing about me.'

'Mrs Farooq says we must stay strong to our values in Ireland,' Mother says.

Mrs Farooq has far too much to say, I think. 'Are those her words or yours?'

'Listen to you!' Mother says. 'You're already more outspoken. You're not a good respectful girl any longer.'

'We'll talk later.' I snatch up my bag of books.

'Sharnaz would never speak to me in such a way.'

Her words are like a knife in my belly. I stop rushing for the bus. I stand in front of Mother. Look into her eyes.

'I love you and respect you with all my heart, Mother,' I tell her. 'You are my world. I always wish love and blessings on you. But I'm not Sharnaz and I never will be.'

She strokes my face and smiles at me as her tears come. 'I don't want you to be Sharnaz. I love you as you are.'

I kiss her cheek. 'See you later.'

I take the stairs two at a time: the bus never waits and school is too far to walk. Seán's revving the engine. He never turns it off. He makes out he's going to pull out any second, then sits with the engine idling for half an hour. People hurry down the steps, pulling on jackets, dragging kids, holding bits of toast, only for Seán to sit for another ten minutes. I've also seen him pull away as someone comes rushing out the door. This morning, I'm the last student on.

'Eight fifteen!' Seán taps his watch face, warning me. 'Just made it.'

Once I'm in, empty seats are filled by a handful of people

hitching a lift into town. With the Centre so far out, spare bus seats are snapped up by people looking for a lift: first come first served. Seán charges them for the lift.

'No standing! No standing!' he shouts, looking down the bus through his mirror. 'No seat, no lift. Get off the bus.'

We get around his rules by cramming three to a seat, six or even seven along the back row. I squash in beside a woman with a little boy on her knee.

Seán shuts the door, throws the bus into gear and we're off.

I daydream out the window and think about Mother's words: *Sharnaz would never speak to me in such a way.* I was never like my sister; Mother knows this. Sharnaz was obedient, respectful, well behaved. I was always in trouble. I was the one Mother had to remind about my behaviour. Always up to mischief. It was me who climbed the tree to pick green mangoes, while Sharnaz held the basket below to catch them. It was me who fell into the water at the washing stones while Sharnaz knelt on the bank, holding her sides laughing. Mother knows I am not anything like my beautiful sister, yet somehow she's making out I should be.

She has too much time to think. And now she has too much time to listen to Mrs Farooq. Back in our village, Mother was busy running the house from before dawn. She worked all day until sundown without needing to sleep. That was too much; she needed to rest a little, but since coming here, she has so little to do and spends her time feeling exhausted. Thoughts go around and around in her head endlessly, which isn't good. And now she has the ultra-conservative Orthodox Mrs Farooq giving her views on everything.

Later that day and earlier than expected, my signs of being a woman appear. I'm not prepared and have no rag with me. In the school bathroom, a girl around my own age is washing her hands. She watches in the mirror as I take a bundle of handtowels to use as protection. I'm immediately ashamed, but I've no choice.

She's still there when I come out of the cubicle. It's like she's waiting for me, which worries me. I try to remember if she's the girl who told me to go back to the African jungle, but I don't think so.

'It's really crap when you don't have money for stuff, isn't it?' the girl says. 'You know you can get proper supplies for free in the library?'

I'm mortified. I've never spoken to any woman other than Mother and Sharnaz about being unclean. But I'm curious about what this girl is saying. What does she mean 'proper supplies'? Doesn't every woman use a rag?

'In the library?' I ask.

'Just ask for the key to the women's toilets,' the girl says. 'They keep it stocked so you can take what you need.' I'm squirming inside so much I can hardly look at her, but there's not a trace of embarrassment in her face. It must not be shameful to talk about this in Ireland.

'You can also get a free packet of supplies every week in the big supermarket out on the Wexford Road,' she continues. 'But you have to sign up for their app first.'

Free packet? Sign up? App? All this new information is dizzying. It means nothing to me.

'Thanks,' I reply.

'No bother. I'm Emer, by the way. I see you most days coming out of the resource room with other girls. You're not in my year, are you?'

'Azari,' I say. 'First year.'

'You look older than first year.'

'I'm in a younger class to catch up,' I explain. 'My English isn't good.'

Emer laughs. 'I'd say that's a whole lot of fun – hanging around with first years!'

I smile. She's friendly.

'If you're interested in knowing more than first years, we've a lunchtime book club. Mainly third years but there's a couple of others in it,' Emer says. 'First Thursday of the month. Would you come along? Might help your English.'

I'm not sure what a book club does, but it sounds a lot like more school. I've enough school already, what with ordinary classes, resource classes and then work-at-home. And anyway, if I feel ashamed in front of younger girls, imagine how I might feel in front of older girls, all doing harder schoolwork.

'I'm not good at reading,' I say.

'We read books about other countries,' Emer says. 'To find out about different places and people. You could tell us about books from your country.'

I smile and shake my head.

'Maybe come to one meeting and see how you feel then?' Emer says.

She's genuine. Really trying to be friendly. The principal told me to find my place, to find friends I can trust. I've not done either yet, but maybe this is one way, though I'll have to find out first what a book club does.

'Maybe one meeting,' I say.

．　　．　　．

I go to the library most days after school. It's warm and quiet and a good place to hide out until the five o'clock Centre bus. Some kids from the Centre hang around the shops with friends or collect younger brothers and sisters from primary school. Most days, I see two black girls waiting at the boys' school to meet up with three black boys. They go down by the river. The primary school kids stay on in the after-school club until it's time for the bus.

Today, three Irish girls from my class are in the library, books, copies and phones on the table. They're not usually here. Must be working on a project. They stop their chat when they see me. Stare as I pass. One of them smiles at me but turns away when the others whisper to her. They burst out laughing. Emer's words come back to me: *I'd say that's a whole lot of fun – hanging around with first years!* I smile to myself as I stop at the desk to ask for the toilet key.

The shelf in the toilet is stocked with different products I've never seen before. Packets and wrappers. I look at them, read the leaflets on the shelf next to them, see a notice telling me to take what I need. Even though I'm alone, my face burns from the embarrassment of seeing them on display, alongside notices and leaflets – so different to anything I ever learned. At home, a woman's time of impurity is secretive. Never to be discussed. We're unclean. Shameful. We hide away. Follow rules and rituals. But here in Ireland, there are free products, signs, information on show for anyone to see. I put some of the products in my schoolbag, along with leaflets to read later.

I return the key and make for the row of chairs at the end of the library. Taking out my English book, I try to read, but don't get far. My head is buzzing with thoughts of Emer and the leaflets and the free supplies and a book club. So many new things to think about!

A pair of boots stop in front of me. Scuffed and battered.

'Hiya,' says a boy's voice. 'I seen you before.'

I look up. A lanky boy stands before me. Bleached hair. Grin. He smiles. 'D'you speak English?'

I glance back to the local girls. Must be a set-up with one of their mates. To my surprise, they're not even looking in our direction.

The boy dumps his schoolbag on the floor. Sits in the chair next to mine. He glances at the book open on my lap. 'Your book's English, so I guess the answer is yes. Yep, I definitely seen you before.'

I can smell his hair product. His body spray. I've never been alone in a boy's company before. He makes me nervous. I glance towards the librarian's desk.

'Are you a runner? You look like a runner.'

He's got my attention now. I look closely at him. Silver nose stud. Eyebrow ring.

'I'm Robert. I'm a runner. I come to the library to do me homework sometimes. And I download their audiobooks for me long runs. Ever try them?'

'Long runs?' I say.

He laughs. 'No. Audiobooks. They're great. Much better than trying to read them anyways.'

I nod at his nose stud. 'We're not allowed jewellery in our school.'

He grins. 'Them nuns up in St Mary's is real strict. Community college is more relaxed. Jewellery and stuff is OK. D'you have to leave all your savage jewellery at home? You know, them bangles and anklets n bells n all. Did I tell you I'm Robert?'

'You did. And that you're a runner. I'm Azari.' I shouldn't be talking to him alone. I start gathering up my things. 'I'd better go.'

'Already?'

He's nice to chat to. Friendly. But what would Mother say? What would Mrs Farooq say? It's disrespectful when I'm unaccompanied. And boys aren't safe.

I slide my book into my bag.

'You're not from around here,' Robert says. 'Does everyone run where you come from?'

'The girls' school had a running club.'

'And the boys?'

I think of my little brothers at home. What they spend every minute of their free time doing. 'Cricket. Boys play a lot of cricket.'

'Deadly.' Robert smiles. 'I know nothing about cricket. What did you do as well as running?'

Mother taught Sharnaz and me how to blend spices and herbs to enrich stews and fried dishes. We grilled flatbread every morning and made yogurt from goat's milk. Homemade cheese. I haven't tasted our traditional foods since leaving home. I miss the flavours so much.

'Food,' I tell Robert. 'I liked to cook spicy dishes.'

'Oh I love me food,' Robert says. 'I do love a spice bag on a Friday night.' He smiles again. 'Tell us about your running, Azari.'

'I ran as much as I could. And then I stopped.'

'And now that you're running here, is it the same?'

Is it the same? *Nothing* is the same, I want to tell this Robert. I also want to tell him:

- I don't run as much as I'd like
- Father stopped me running, Mother wants to stop me running
- I feel ashamed as a girl in tight clothes
- I'm nervous outside on my own
- Running is freedom to me. Running is *everything* to me.

I also want to tell him sometimes I run to get out of the craziness of the Centre, to get out of my head. It gives me a break from being with my mother all the time, which isn't good for either of us, but Mother doesn't see it that way, and then I'm guilty for thinking it. She wants me with her all day, every day. And that's not what I want. But I've only just met Robert. Putting those words together is too difficult for me. I didn't even realise I had so many answers in my head to such a short question. I blink.

''Tis a bit,' I say.

'I'm in a running club,' Robert says. 'At the GAA. You're not a member there, are you?'

'Miss Cullen's?'

'The very one. PE teacher in your school, isn't she?'

'I'm not a member,' I say.

'You should join,' Robert says. 'It's great craic. You meet loads of runners.'

I stand up. Swing my bag on my shoulder. 'I have to go. Nice to meet you, Robert.'

'See you, Azari.'

.　　.　　.

I try to get Mother out at weekends when the weather is fine, even for a short walk, but she always has excuses: her bones can't take it. Her head hurts. She's too tired. The Centre and her tormented thoughts are her entire world. We stay in our room most evenings after dinner. She lies in bed, sometimes sleeping, sometimes staring at the wall, sometimes talking. This evening, she wants to talk.

'How do you think our boys are doing, Azari?' she asks. 'I hope they're still at school.'

'Aunt Hania will make sure of it. She'll send them with her boys.'

She gives a little smile. 'Five boys under one roof. Imagine how noisy their house is – Poor Hania. Poor Iman. I miss them so much.'

I know what's coming next. We've had this conversation many times since we got to Ireland. It never gets any easier.

'It's not right they're growing up without me,' Mother says. Tears shine in her eyes. 'No mother to mind them. To keep them safe and clean.'

'They'll be safe with Aunt Hania,' I say. 'She has Iman to help her.'

'They're still so young.' Her tears are flowing freely now. 'And they were so frightened of your father before we left. His temper. His anger.' She turns to me, her eyes stricken. 'He won't have harmed them, will he?'

I don't know, I think. After all that happened, I don't know what my father might be capable of. But I don't say that to Mother. 'Aunt Hania will make sure they're safe. She'll mind them.'

'I left them behind. I put you ahead of them. I put *me* ahead of them. That's not right. I left my babies. I should have stayed. I should never have abandoned them.' She reaches for my hand. 'I don't mean you're less important: I didn't want to choose between any of you. I love you all equally.'

I stroke her hair. 'I know you do.'

'I'm too hard on you, Azari,' she says.

'How so?'

'When you aren't here during the day and I only have my thoughts for company, I think over things I've said to you and feel such guilt.' Mother pushes herself up on her elbow. 'About your running, I mean. I'm trying my best to keep you safe and protected, to make sure you're a respectable young woman. I know you're already that – you're a good daughter. And I know in my heart your running won't change that.'

I smile at her. 'Are you coming around to my running? Are you saying it's OK now?'

'It's never OK.' She smiles, even though her eyes are sad. 'But you need something other than school and this Centre. Something to keep you busy. Running is important to you. I don't want you to stop.'

This is a big change for Mother. It must have been a difficult decision, especially in the face of Mrs Farooq's disapproval.

'Where did this change of heart come from?' I ask her.

'I don't want you to have to choose between running and me.' She sighs. 'I might lose that battle.'

'You won't lose me,' I say. 'But thank you, Mother. That means a lot to me.'

'Of course, Mrs Farooq doesn't agree with my view.'

'No surprise there. But you don't have to feel guilty.'

She lies down again. 'I feel guilt and remorse about so many things in my life. Oh Azari, I should never have abandoned my youngest chicks. Musa was terrified of your father, and as for Kashif, he's such a sensitive little boy.'

'You didn't abandon them, Mother,' I say, thinking of Musa and Kashif. How young they are. Tears sting my eyes. I blink them away. 'We had to leave. We had to run for our lives,

Mother. And we're doing what Sharnaz wanted. Bringing the boys was impossible.'

Mother will take her broken heart to the grave. I sit next to her, soothing her and letting her rest. What happened back home is eating her up inside. Eventually, she drifts off to sleep and I sit quietly, thinking of my little brothers. Praying that Aunt Hania did indeed take them to live with her. My thoughts turn to Mother's words, and I feel warm inside at how she has given me permission to keep running.

I pull out the leaflets I picked up in the library. Read through them slowly. They tell me things I never knew about my own body. How it works. How I'm not unclean or impure, although that's still how I think of it. I open the packets and wrappers. Look at the products. Think about how this changes everything I thought I knew. And how I might change what I do from now on. So much to think about!

Then of course, there's the boy in the library. He had a friendly face. I liked talking to him. I liked his smile. But Mother, Sharnaz, Father, the village women, the Farooqs, in fact, probably every person I have ever known, would tell me no respectable woman should be alone with a boy. Men take a woman's honour. What does this boy Robert want from me? He's friendly. He came over to talk. I don't think he wants to hurt me, but I'm not sure. I've never before spoken to a man outside my family – other than my coach, and Jalal in the factory. I can't ask Mother about him. She's so afraid of Irish boys, she'll want to take me back to the village to marry me off. Mrs Farooq would collapse on the spot if I even mentioned men. She would have to get her perfect daughter – Fiza? – disinfected and quarantined if she happened to hear an Irish boy had spoken to me. There's only one person I can think of to talk to about it.

Next day, I find the tall, stately woman, Princess. She hoots with laughter, shaking so much her bright orange headscarf works itself loose and she has to tie it up again. Her silvery hoop earrings tremble in her ears. This wasn't the reaction I expected.

'You've never spoken to a boy before? *Ever?*'

'They're not safe,' I tell her. 'It's not right to be alone with a boy.'

Princess tries to be serious but her mouth twitches at the corners.

'Sure, *some* men are not safe,' she says. 'And boys can be rough and stupid at times, but not *all* men and boys are not safe and not *all* the time.' Her eyes sparkle as she looks at me. 'This Robert – what did you talk about?'

'Mostly running.'

'In the library? In broad daylight?' She smiles. 'What did you think he might do?'

'I didn't wait to find out,' I say.

'He came up to chat with you and you walked out?'

'I didn't walk out. We talked. I left for the bus. What if I was seen talking alone to him? It was disrespectful.'

'In your home, it might be disrespectful, but in Ireland and many other countries, it's not disrespectful for a boy and girl to talk alone in the library,' Princess says.

'You sure?'

'I'm very sure. Sounds like he was friendly. No harm in that. We all need friends. The more we have, the better. Young friends, old friends, friends like us, and friends different from us. They make our lives richer and more interesting.' She smiles widely at me. 'It's good to have a new friend, Azari-Nike.'

Chapter 6

It was days before Mother told Sharnaz and me what Uncle Rashid and the village council wanted with Father.

'Your uncle's debt must be paid. He has no money. Your father has no money. The council has decided.'

Sharnaz gripped my hand as Mother continued.

'Sharnaz will be settlement to Abbas Sharif instead of payment.'

'No, Mother!' Sharnaz cried out.

'What does that mean?' I looked at Mother. At Sharnaz.

Tears brimmed in Sharnaz's eyes. She shook her head: no, no, no. 'Please, Mother.'

'We must all do our duty,' Mother said. 'It will cancel the debt. Order will be restored.'

'What's going on?' I asked.

Sharnaz whipped around to me. 'Marriage! That's what. I've been promised in marriage to an old man.'

'Is that true?' I said to Mother. I felt sick to my stomach.

'Everyone agreed,' said Mother. 'The Sharifs. The council. Your father.'

'What about me?' Sharnaz whispered. 'Everyone agreed, but what about me? I'm fifteen, Mother.'

She was up off her knees and out to Father under the mango tree. We tried to stop her, but she was too quick. She crouched at his knee, pleading with him. We listened and watched from behind the curtains. My heart beat fast.

'Please don't do this, Father,' Sharnaz sobbed. 'Abbas Sharif has three daughters older than me.'

'It's done,' Father said.

'He has grandchildren. He's an old man, Father.' Tears ran down Sharnaz's face. 'I'm too young.'

'Men's business,' Father said. 'The council has agreed. It doesn't concern you.'

'I'm a good daughter, Father. I work hard. Bring home good money.'

I could see Father getting angry. I was afraid to move. I willed Sharnaz to say nothing. She sank down and covered her face.

'I can't do this, Father,' she said. 'I'm sorry.'

He struck her across the face. She never saw it coming and was flung back onto the dirt. Even still, Sharnaz refused to give in.

'I won't marry him.'

Father swung his leg and kicked her hard in the ribs, pitching her onto her side. Sharnaz gasped and curled up on the ground.

He swung another kick, smashing into her ribs again. Sharnaz screamed and lurched on the ground.

'How dare you,' he said.

We shrank back when he stormed into the house. Father grabbed Mother's hair. Twisted it around his fist, jerking her head so she had to look up at him.

'This is your doing,' he snarled. His spit flecked her face. 'With your notions of education for her. She'll do her duty, or you'll have me to answer to.'

He flung her away and stormed out of the house.

I rushed to Mother's side. She waved me away. 'I'm fine. See to your sister.'

I ran to Sharnaz, who was clutching her side. Gasping for breath. She whimpered and twisted. I crouched next to her. Stroked her hair. Held her hand. Mother followed me out. My sister screamed in pain when Mother touched her ribs.

'I think they're broken,' Mother said.

I fetched hot water and cloths. Mother bound Sharnaz's ribs and I held a damp cloth over her eye, already swollen from Father's strike. She lay quietly and allowed us to tend her, only getting upset again when we finished.

'I can't. I can't.' Sobs knotted her words. 'Not an old man. Six grandchildren. A widower longer than I'm alive.'

'Hush now,' Mother said. She stroked her hair, smoothing it away from her forehead. 'Don't get upset. We'll get through this. Don't cry.'

'No, no, no,' Sharnaz kept saying. 'I'm not ready. I will never be ready for him.' She lifted her head and looked at

Mother, wincing with pain. 'I can't. Don't make me, Mother. Talk to Father.'

Mother kept up her soothing words, her comforting touch. Sharnaz stopped talking and fell silent. Mother murmured to her, caring and loving. She said words Sharnaz wanted to hear, but she never once said the marriage wouldn't go ahead. She never promised Sharnaz would stay home, safe and unmarried with us. We knew nothing would change what my father and the village council had agreed. The bargain had been struck. The marriage would go ahead.

It was dark when we helped Sharnaz into the house. She whimpered when she tried to stand, leaning on my arm to protect her broken ribs. We laid her gently on the charpoy. Afraid of causing her more pain, I lay on the floor, but couldn't sleep. It seemed I had only shut my eyes when Mother lit the charcoal for breakfast. I washed my face. Brushed my hair.

'Go on your own today,' Mother told me. 'Say Sharnaz is ill. That she'll be back in a day or so.'

It was strange and frightening walking alone through the dark village to the bus stop. I had never been without Sharnaz and didn't feel safe. I kept looking back to make sure I wasn't being followed. A couple of men at the water pump stopped to watch me, making comments under their breath. They followed me with their eyes. I sprinted the last part, fast as I could, only slowing down when I saw other women waiting for the bus.

On the way to the factory, all I could think of was Sharnaz and the old man she would marry. As the bus rocked along the narrow roads, I dozed off. A woman nudged me awake when we reached the bus station.

Sharnaz's supervisor was furious when I told him she was ill.

'Who's going to do her work – are you?' he shouted. 'How am I to fill orders if she's not here?'

I didn't know what to say.

'Tell her if she's not back tomorrow, she's out!' he said.

I fled to my own section where Jalal cuffed me on the ear for being late. 'Lazy dog! Get a move on.'

All morning, I fretted for Sharnaz. What if she couldn't return to work the next day? I didn't know how long it took broken ribs to heal, but I didn't think they'd be better by then. What if she lost her job? Father would be enraged with her, even though he caused it. But he would never see it that way. He would say she brought it on herself by her insolence. At lunchtime, I slipped down to the yard as usual, squatting in the shade on my own to eat flatbread.

Komal joined me. 'They can't fire her for one day's sick leave. Her job is safe.'

'I don't know when she'll be back,' I said.

'Is it bad?'

I nodded. I wasn't sure how much to tell Komal. Would I be betraying my father? Shaming my family? We all knew girls in worse situations: Deeba worked long hours in the kilns to pay her family's debts. Her little sisters scavenged alone in the rubbish dump. But it didn't make it right to tell my family's story.

'Your father?' Komal asked.

I nodded.

'Is she badly hurt?'

I checked there was nobody close by before I replied. 'Broken ribs. Black eye.'

'Is she at home?'

'Where else?'

It was another two days before Sharnaz returned to work. She could hardly walk, holding her side to protect her ribs. She kept her head down, her scarf pulled across her bruised eye. At lunchtime, I searched for her, but couldn't find her or Komal anywhere.

'Is Sharnaz around?' I asked one of the girls in her section.

She shrugged. 'Try the yard.'

They weren't in the yard. I ate my flatbread alone and returned to work.

At the end of the day, Sharnaz was sitting on the wall outside.

'What are you doing?' I asked.

'Waiting for you.'

'I looked for you at lunchtime.' I was vexed. All day I'd been worrying and here she was sitting in the sun.

'The supervisor wanted to see me,' Sharnaz said.

'About your job? Did they fire you?' My irritation was forgotten.

'I'm working in quality control for a few weeks until I'm healed.'

'You still have your job?'

We walked slowly towards the bus station.

'Komal came with me to help, as the labour union leader. She was brilliant.' Sharnaz looked at me. 'They can't fire me because of my rights, Azari. I never knew what rights meant before but now I understand. Komal explained them to me.'

'Is quality control easier?'

'It's not so painful sitting down,' Sharnaz said.

But Komal and workers' rights and working in quality control couldn't help with Sharnaz's arranged marriage. From the day Father broke the news to Mother, it was like a light died in my sister. The bruises faded, her ribs healed, but her spirit was broken. No matter what time I woke during the night, she was awake, staring out the broken window at the moonlight. Nothing I said brought a smile to her lips. She hardly ate, only picking at her food at home when Mother encouraged her, or Father told her not to waste good food. She insisted I take her flatbread and eggs at lunchtime. She grew thin and pale.

.   .   .

Wedding preparations had started. The first ceremony marked the engagement. Abbas Sharif and his family came to our house. I hadn't seen him up close before and didn't at first realise the bent-over man helped by his eldest daughter into our yard was to be my sister's husband. Wiry and wizened, with hairy ears and yellow finger-nails, he didn't take his beady eyes off Sharnaz throughout the ceremony. We sat apart from the Sharif clan during the engagement ceremony, as was the custom. Sharnaz didn't speak a word, her head draped with a hand-beaded silk scarf, so her face wasn't visible. Father fulfilled the formal requirements. A date for the wedding was agreed.

Once the engagement ceremony was over, things started to happen fast. I felt nervous whenever something to do with the wedding arrived at our home: gold rings, necklaces, gold anklets with tiny bells, hanks of brightly coloured silks for our dresses, hand-painted dishes and bowls. Our outfits for the various ceremonies were agreed. The dressmaker measured us all. She took away the silks to cut and stitch. Father decided the menu. Ordered and paid for the goat to be slaughtered and prepared. There was so much to be arranged: musicians, drummers, dancers, outfits, food, lamps, fireworks.

As soon as she was married, Sharnaz would leave our home and the factory to work in the Sharif household and farm.

The pre-wedding ceremony was only days away. We borrowed silk cushions for the henna party and the wedding ceremony. We swept the yard and adorned the mango tree with little lights and ribbons. Tiny honey sweets studded with dried fruits and dusted with fine sugar arrived from the Sharif household in a ribboned gift box. Platters of fruit, nuts and pastries were delivered. The evening of the henna party, Mother and I washed and combed Sharnaz's glossy hair. She was pale and silent, her skin like ice. She kept her eyes down.

The women from the village gathered in our yard as sunlight faded and everything turned hazy and blue. They brought flowers and yellow candles in little clay pots, which they set around where Sharnaz sat on cushions under the mango tree. She looked beautiful in her silk gown and gold jewellery, surrounded by blossoms, little flames flickering like stars in the dusk and gleaming in the eyes of everyone around her. Aunt

Hania painted henna designs on Sharnaz's hands, fingers and toes. Once she was done, Aunt Hania painted our guests' hands. There was laughter and excitement as the women chose their designs and twisted their decorated hands in the air. I brought Sharnaz little sweets on a silver dish and knelt next to her.

'Tomorrow is the end of my life,' she whispered.

'I'll pray he gets a heart-attack and dies,' I whispered back.

Sharnaz gave a sad little smile and held my hand in her icy one.

. . .

The next morning, I rose in darkness to light the charcoal in the little brazier. There was the promise of dawn in the sky, an early mist in the yard. The air felt cool. Everyone was asleep except Sharnaz, who was already up and gone to the outhouse. Mother followed her while I boiled water and started breakfast. I woke the boys.

'Get Mother and Sharnaz,' I said to Kashif. 'Breakfast is ready.'

He scampered across the yard but was back in moments. 'They're not there.'

I looked at him. 'Neither of them? Did you open the outhouse?'

'I looked. They're not there.' He ran off.

I crossed the yard to check myself. The outhouse was empty.

Father came out of the house, scratching his belly and farting. 'Where's your mother?'

'Gone down the village with Sharnaz,' I lied.

I scurried from the yard as Father crossed to the outhouse.

Out on the lane, smoke from cooking fires hung in the early morning air. Cocks crowed. A dog barked. I walked to the corner. In the distance, Mother hurried towards me, alone. Her eyes were wide, her headscarf pulled a little to one side.

'I can't find her,' she said when she reached where I stood.

'Where did you look?'

'Market square. When did you speak to her?'

'I didn't,' I said. 'She was already out. I thought she was washing.'

'You didn't see her at all?'

Something cold and tight settled in my stomach. 'She can't be far. She'll be back soon.'

'Don't tell your father,' Mother said.

Sharnaz hadn't returned by the time breakfast was finished. Father hadn't asked; he must've thought she was busy with wedding preparations.

'Go to work,' Mother said to me. 'See if you can find her,' she whispered.

I hurried to catch the bus, looking for Sharnaz as I ran. The women on the bus were full of chat about the wedding, asking me questions. Excited about the three-day celebrations in the village. I smiled and joked with them, but in my head, I fretted about Sharnaz. As the bus travelled to town, I checked side roads and fields for signs of my sister.

Once I got to the factory, I hurried first to Sharnaz's section.

'Have you seen Sharnaz?' I asked some of the girls. I made my voice bright, but they were suspicious straight away.

'What's wrong? What's happened?'

'Nothing,' I said. 'She's around somewhere.'

They knew something was amiss; I heard them whispering as I hurried to my section.

Komal followed me. 'Is there a problem?'

I didn't want to bring shame on my family, even with Komal. 'I think she's gone to buy some last-minute items.'

The morning lasted for ever. I couldn't focus on my work. Jalal cursed me. Called my family bad names.

'I'm ready to throw you out on the street,' he said, tearing another spoiled garment from my shaking hands. 'Thank the stars you're only working until lunchtime today.'

At lunchtime, I left the factory early for the pre-wedding ceremonies. There was no sign of Sharnaz anywhere in the factory, the bus station, or on the way home. As I walked through the village, I was sick with fear and worry.

Father grabbed me as soon as I entered our yard. 'Where is she?'

'I don't know, Father.' My voice trembled.

He struck me across the face with the back of his fist. I crashed to the dirt, raising my hand to protect myself from the next blow, but it never came.

'Don't lie to me.' He spat the words out. 'Where have you hidden her?'

'I don't know where she is, Father. I haven't seen her.'

'Did you help her?'

'No, Father. I've been looking for her.'

'Then keep looking!'

Mother and I hunted everywhere we could think of: the school, Ruba and Deeba's homes, the market. Down by the river, the washing stones, the back laneways, the rubbish dump, the pool where boys swam, the sacred pool thick with water lilies. People stood in the street watching us. Whispering to each other. They guessed what had happened. Old women covered their faces and muttered about shame and honour. The more we searched, the more frantic we became. She couldn't have vanished into thin air. It was a small village.

'She doesn't want to be found,' I said to Mother.

It was early evening when we returned home, exhausted and downbeat. There was nowhere we hadn't already tried a hundred times. We crept into the yard where Father paced. The boys hid in the house.

Ceremonies were due to start shortly. The yard was already decorated with coloured ribbons, flowers and the little pots of candles but nothing else was ready. No platters of sweets or drinks were laid out. No softly glowing lanterns. None of us was dressed in our wedding clothes. The fire pit to roast the meat wasn't even lit. These were all the jobs that should have been done in the afternoon while we ran through the streets searching for my sister.

Sharnaz's beautiful embroidered dress and jewellery hung inside, along with the silk cushions and jewelled headscarves. The musicians and drummers were due to arrive soon; then locals would trickle in, expecting an evening of celebration and festivities.

The Sharif clan were holding their own pre-wedding ceremony, so we would be spared the shame of their company. All was not lost. Although the Sharifs would surely hear of this afterwards, we might still save face if Sharnaz could be found and the ceremony went ahead. But I wasn't hopeful.

Father looked at us as we trailed into the yard. He spat, then stalked out. As he passed the mango tree, he tore down a handful of coloured ribbons, grinding them into the dirt.

Nobody arrived for the pre-wedding ceremony. Half the village already knew Sharnaz had gone missing and word was passed around the other half. The musicians didn't arrive, although Father would still have to pay them. Mother and I packed away the fruit, nuts and pastries in silence. We folded Sharnaz's dress and jewellery into a box and stored it out of sight. Mother sent the boys to take in the lanterns and ribbons. We spoke in whispers all evening and crept around.

There was no sign of Father or Sharnaz by the time we were ready to sleep.

Chapter 7

For the first time since coming to Ireland, I've things to think about other than life in our little village and Mother and international protection. When I get to school a few days' later, a folded-over sheet of paper is on my chair.

'An older girl came looking for you,' a classmate tells me. 'She knew your name, so I showed her your desk.'

I read the note:

Book club meeting - Thursday week. School library, 1.00pm. Maybe we'll see you? Told the others you're coming. Everyone dying to meet you. Emer

I feel a mixture of happiness and excitement, and a sudden rush of nerves. What's going to happen at the book club? What am I expected to do? As I hurry to the resource room later, I'm distracted about the book club, wondering how it works. I'm not paying attention and collide straight into a knot of girls chatting on the corridor.

'Sorry,' I say.

One of them shoves me back and glares at me. She's Irish and she's angry.

'Bloody fugee! Watch where you're going, right?'

I try to get past, but they block my way.

'Them parasites can't even walk down a corridor like normal people,' says another Irish girl. I recognise her as the one who said I couldn't speak English. She makes a sudden lunge for me. I jump back, dropping my books and pens, which clatter to the ground. The girls kick them across the floor, laughing. One of the girls whips her phone out to film what's happening.

'Sponger! Don't even know why you get free handouts – can't even read books.'

'Go on back to where you came from, bleedin' scrounger.'

'Freeloader!'

'Girls!' It's the resource teacher. '*What* is going on here?'

She looks from me to the group of girls and back at me.

'This girl dropped her books, Miss,' says the girl who lunged at me. 'We were just helping her pick them up, Miss.'

'That's not what it looked or sounded like to me,' says the resource teacher.

'Swear to God, Miss,' says the girl with the phone, which is out of sight now. 'That's all that happened.'

They collect up my books, give them to the girl who started it off. She comes over to me, really close. Slams my books against me as she's handing them over. Her eyes screw up as she stares at me. 'Rat us out and I'll bleedin' burst you later, you hear, fugee?'

The resource teacher doesn't believe me when I tell her nothing happened.

'I know those girls, Azari. And they weren't helping you pick up your books. If you tell me what they said and what went on, I can help you.'

I shake my head. 'It's OK, Miss. Nothing happened.'

She goes easy on me that day and by the time class is over, I'm over the shakes. I'm wary coming out of the resource room but I don't see any of the girls and I make sure to pay attention for the rest of the day.

·   ·   ·

In the library after school, my thoughts turn to Robert and what Princess said about him just being friendly. But Sharnaz has a different view. In my head, she warns: *Be careful with a boy, Azari! Don't damage your chances of a good marriage. That's what boys do.*

'He was genuine, Sharnaz. He wasn't interested in *me*. He was friendly and chatty.'

I wish she was here, so she could meet him, but that can't be. I console myself with talking to her in my head. *What will you tell Mother?* Sharnaz asks.

'I don't know. She would have a heart-attack if she knew.'

That he's a boy?

That he's a white boy?

That he's a white Irish boy?

'I know! I know! Everything about him is wrong. I can't possibly tell her. Why can't he be a brown girl from our village who loves running?'

But I forget all about bullies and book clubs and Robert when I arrive back to the Centre and find Mother in the corridor outside our room, her hands on her hips. Her eyes are bulging. She's furious.

'What is it?' I say.

She waves her arms towards the open door. 'Someone else in the room. A new person.'

'In our room?'

'Look!' Mother says.

Our room looks completely different than this morning. It's an even bigger mess. Our big bed has been pushed up against the wall, under the window. Against the other wall is a new narrow bed, heaped high with plastic bags spilling over with clothes and shoes. Black bin-liners are stacked on the floor, splitting open.

'Who owns all that?' I ask.

'The manager came,' Mother says. 'I hid under the blankets. He used his key. Walked right in.'

The manager unlocks bedroom doors and walks in any time he wants, no asking. No permission. People are always complaining about it. He says he's checking for prohibited items and rule-breakers, but it's not respectful or proper, especially for a woman on her own like Mother.

'He talked and talked,' Mother says. 'I didn't understand. He took our clothes from the drawers, put them on the bed.

I thought he was throwing us out. I pushed him out. Shut the door.'

I look at Mother with respect. She rarely stands up for herself, yet she pushed the manager out of the room. 'What happened then?'

'He came back later with two staff and a new bed,' she said. 'They moved our bed. Put in that one.'

I look at our clothes and personal belongings, pulled from the drawers and heaped on our bed. Only half the floor has lino on it. Now our bed's been moved, there are bare floorboards, dirty and stained, with no lino.

The bathroom door on the landing opens and a white woman comes out. She is short. Solid. She passes us and walks into *our* room, stomping like she has weights on her feet.

'*She* arrived after lunch,' Mother whispers.

I stare at the woman, then follow her. She opens and closes *our* drawers until she finds an empty one, into which she shoves an armful of clothing. She straightens up when I come in.

'Meri,' she says, pointing to herself. She points to the new bed. 'Meri's bed.' She points to our bed. 'Your bed.'

She pushes past me and waves at Mother, still on the corridor.

'Come, come,' she says, inviting Mother into her own room. *Our* room.

She turns to her bed and pushes a heap of the clothes and bags onto the floor, making everything a whole lot worse.

'Sorry,' she says. She points to herself. 'Meri! Meri! You?'

'Azari,' I say.

Mother says nothing. She folds her arms across her chest and turns her back on Meri, which says a lot more than any words.

I complain to the manager about overcrowding and no privacy and sharing with foreign strangers. Princess comes with me to help me find the right words.

'It's allowed.' The manager waves the rule book in our faces. 'It's in the book. Look it up!'

'We need a bigger room,' I say. 'It's too small for three people.'

'A family of two and a stranger,' Princess says. 'Not good enough.'

'You want a bigger room?' says the manager. 'Fine. I'll give you a bigger room. Share with five strangers instead of one in a bigger room. See how you like it then.'

We appeal to the government officials, like the rule books tell you, but nobody answers Princess's emails.

'They always win,' says Princess. 'They're the government. They do as they like.'

.   .   .

From then on, we share our room with Meri, but that's where her sharing stops. She doesn't share the food she keeps in plastic bags under her bed. She doesn't share the lemonade bottles of dark liquid she hides in the back of the cupboard.

'Alcohol,' Mother whispers to me.

Food and drink are not allowed in the rooms. No smoking. No alcohol. Meri doesn't care. She keeps snacks and drink under the bed. Munches her way through crackers at night.

The bedroom was small to begin with, but it's a whole lot smaller now. We try to make space for her stuff. She has a lot of it. She spreads everywhere. Wherever her things land is fine by her. She takes over a shelf in the wardrobe, then two shelves, sometimes all three until Mother empties Meri's stuff onto her bed and it starts again: the silent battle between them.

Meri and Mother hardly have a sentence of English between them, so when I'm in the room, I spend my time translating our language into my version of English. I'm not sure how Meri's brain translates my English into her own language, but it gets scrambled somehow because everything I tell her results in snorts and shrugs. She has an intense stare. Round black eyes bore into me like hot marbles until I have to look away. It must not be rude to stare in her country.

Meri comes from some country that used to be part of a bigger country but now is independent and at war with the bigger country. It doesn't take her long to find others in the Centre who speak her language. She brings them to our room to share the food and drink she never shares with us. Three, sometimes four, women cram onto Meri's bed to talk and drink alcohol and eat. They eat crackers and packets of buns. Crumbs all over the floor and on the bed. They laugh and talk louder as the bottle empties.

Tonight is one of those nights.

I take my books and pens downstairs to find somewhere to do my work-at-home. The TV room is full of families watching a comedy. Kids are laughing and shouting at the movie. Mother is in the canteen talking to Mrs Farooq, but they'll be moved out soon enough because the canteen is locked once dinner's over.

I end up sitting halfway up the stairs with my schoolbooks on my knee. Someone shouts at three boys wrestling in the lobby. They open the front door and tumble out. A gust of cold air scatters my papers. I grab them, dropping my pen and book. I can't concentrate. I don't understand the English on the page. My head aches.

'Hey, Azari.' Princess comes down the stairs behind me. Tonight, she's wearing a peacock blue dress splashed with scarlet flowers. Her hair is twisted high and wrapped in a matching headscarf. She's wearing bright red lipstick and long bead ear-rings. She squeezes herself on the step right next to me, completely blocking the stairs, but Princess doesn't care.

'School work?' she asks.

'I don't even know what I'm meant to do,' I say.

'Don't get worried, Azari-Nike,' Princess says. 'I can help.'

'Really?'

She reaches across and lifts all my schoolbooks from my lap. Shuts them and slides them into my schoolbag. She hands me the bag.

'There!' she says. 'It's Friday, girl. Forget schoolwork. Come to the TV room instead.'

She stands up and winks at me. 'Come on! You can finish that tomorrow.'

She walks downstairs and disappears into the TV room. That was no help at all. I'm taking my books out of my bag again when Mother comes out of the canteen with Mrs Farooq.

'Queenie wants us to go to the TV room,' she says to me. 'Coming?'

'Queenie? Her name is Princess, Mother.'

'For the meeting,' Mrs Farooq says.

'What meeting?' I ask. 'I never heard about a meeting.'

Meetings are not good news. The manager calls them every few weeks to remind us of the Centre rules:

- · No food in the bedrooms
- · No washing or drying clothes in the bedrooms
- · No visitors after eight o'clock
- · No personal food or baby milk in the kitchen fridge
- · No alcohol

He adds a couple of new ones every time. People complain but he doesn't care.

'You're free to leave any time,' he says. He knows well we've nowhere else to go.

'The manager didn't call the meeting,' Mother says. 'Princess did.'

Is that why she asked me to the TV room? We go to the door. Princess stands in front of the TV.

'We don't want *men*,' she calls out to a couple of men, laughing her deep chuckle. 'This is a *women's* meeting. Out, men, out!'

Some men grumble and give out, but they leave. Nobody stands up to Princess. She's in charge and she knows it. Anyway, she's taller than most of the men in the room. Perhaps they're a little afraid of her.

She turns to a knot of boys sniggering in the corner. 'You too, boys! Out! You're not *women*.'

The boys don't budge from their perch on the corner sofa. They jut their chins out as though daring her. I know most of them from the bus. See them hanging around town after school. Tall and gangly and not fitting into their bodies, they're boys who are almost men and think they own the world. They don't like being bossed around. Princess strides over to them, reaches out a long black arm and grabs the nearest boy by the ear. She frog-marches him towards the door. He whimpers as the women laugh at him and shout support to Princess. One even gives him a wallop on the backside as he's ushered out.

Once he's been evicted, the other boys don't hang around. In a couple of seconds, they're out the door.

Princess spots me standing at the door. 'Azari my friend, come in! Come in! Bring your mother. Join us. This is a women's meeting. We need *all* women. Together we will be *stronger*!'

I'm a little afraid of Princess. How different a country she must come from! In our village, men would beat a woman who stood up to them. Father told us women can't run meetings or make decisions, but the men in Princess's home must think differently. It's a good feeling to see a woman with power. A woman in charge. It's good to be in that room with only women. Mother and I find a seat. Mrs Farooq and Fiza sit on the other side of the room. Fiza catches my eye, a little smile curling her mouth.

Princess strides over to shut the door. We wait. We watch. A couple of dozen women and teenage girls, a few babies and toddlers in arms and on laps. When Princess starts to speak, we stop our whispering and wondering. We listen.

'Welcome to our first meeting,' Princess says. 'We are the women of this Centre. We are the ones who will change things around here.' She looks around. 'We are from ten, fifteen countries. Maybe more.'

We look around at each other. We smile. Nod and agree.

'We're not accustomed to sitting around,' Princess says. 'Not used to being served foreign foods cooked by others. We were busy in our homes. Busy making our own food, running our households.'

'What's she saying?' Mother asks me.

I quickly translate so she can keep up with what's going on. Others do the same for mothers, friends, sisters.

'She doesn't like Irish food?' whispers Mother.

'I don't think she's talking only about Irish food.'

Princess continues. 'We all come from places where we had our own ways, our own foods, our own traditions. We organised our families, prepared meals, went to market. I cooked every day with bitterleaf. Plantain. Waterleaf. Who has seen these in this centre?'

'Fresh coriander,' someone calls out. 'I used fresh coriander all the time.'

'Chilli-fried onions,' says someone else.

'Red chillies,' says a third voice.

Other women call out ingredients from their cooking: Ground-nut oil. Teff. Tofu. Ginger. Sesame. I get lost with the unfamiliar words.

'I think they're all foods,' I tell Mother.

'Green mangoes,' Mother says. She leans forward, smiling at me. 'Tell her we cooked with green mangoes from our tree.'

Green mangoes. Sharnaz and I loved them. All of a sudden, I'm back in our little yard. The hot sun is burning and I'm peering down at Sharnaz through the dark glossy leaves of our tree. I'm surrounded by the scent of mango as I toss them down. Green fruit lands with a thump in the dirt – smooth and perfumed and hard as a stone – and Sharnaz runs to collect them. Mother made spicy mango pickle with garlic, which we ate until our bellies ached. Inside me, a deep yearning opens for my home and my beloved sister and my brothers. For everything I knew in my village.

'I'd forgotten,' I say.

'Tell her,' Mother says.

I tune back to the meeting, but I'm shaken by the intensity of the memory. How quickly I've forgotten details of home.

'Our foods – our *traditional dishes* – are part of who we are,' Princess says. 'They make up our *beings*, our *souls*. They make our hearts beat, our blood run. They are our *essence* from generations back.'

Women shout their support, cheer her words. Tears burn my eyes and I blink them away. I concentrate on translating for Mother.

'We will bring our traditional foods to this place,' Princess says. 'We will cook ourselves happy!'

The door of the TV room bursts open. The manager strides in, his face red.

'This meeting finishes *now*!' he says. 'You have *zero* permission for this carry-on.'

Princess looks at him calmly. 'I don't need your permission to speak freely to my sisters.'

There's a ripple of support from the women, a murmur of voices.

'Taking over the TV room is not allowed,' says the manager. 'I've a young fella here saying he wants to watch TV and you thrun him out.'

The teenager Princess ran out by his ear is standing at the door, grinning from ear to ear.

'This meeting is *over*,' says the manager.

．　　．　　．

I stay within the grounds for my run the next morning, following the same route I did the first time I ran. I want a familiar route, one I don't have to think about. Under the trees. Past the outhouses. Around the fields. I need my body to move without having to think. My head is full of thoughts and memories. I want to give them space. I can't believe I'd forgotten about Sharnaz and me picking mangoes until Mother said it last night. What else is slipping from my memory? Am I going to forget my home? My sister?

I think back to the earliest memory I hold of Sharnaz: we are running side by side towards our father, as fast as our short legs will carry us. We must've been small because he's as tall and bright as the sun, towering above us. The evening light is golden. The heat rises from the dusty street, snatching my breath away. My father smiles broadly in the way I've seen him smile at the boys. It's a long time since he smiled at his daughters that way. He snatches the two of us into his arms and swings us around. I'm laughing so hard I can hardly breathe. I burrow my face into his shoulder and inhale his spicy smoky smell. I cherish the memory as I brush away the tears on my cheeks. I don't want to forget my life before this one. I need to remember it all. Treasure the times we shared together.

Twice around my running route. I push myself faster and faster until I'm breathless and buzzing. My limbs move of their own accord, feeling strong and light. New growth is on the branches and in the dark earth: buds and tiny rolled leaves and little flowers. New life is coming.

Mother and I sleep in the same bed in the Centre because it's the closest I get to sleeping beside Sharnaz. We curl together under the warm covers. I curve around her spine, my body tucked against her. The smell of her, the feel of her body against mine helps me sleep. I miss Sharnaz next to me: the weight of her on the charpoy. The lean of her body. Mother grounds me now Sharnaz isn't here: her arm around me, her leg twined with mine, tethering me to the here and now, stopping my dreams from drifting back to home. Only then does my mind rest, and slowly, sleep seeps into me. I don't tell anybody in Ireland this. I don't think they would understand. It's different here. Girls in school don't share the same closeness with their mothers. They prefer the privacy of their bedrooms. They don't like when their mothers go in uninvited. They watch movies and music and videos on their phones and tablets with the door shut. It's different to what I was used to at home. What do they think their mothers might do? How are they going to learn the most important things about life? About other people?

In our home, there are no separate rooms or shut doors. Mother has life experience: I learn from her. This is the way in my family and in my village: mothers and grandmothers teach daughters and grand-daughters.

When I'm finished my run, I cool down, stretch my muscles, come inside. Heading for the stairs, I glance into the TV room. There are always kids jumping on the sofas or wrestling on the floor, a couple of people watching TV, but today, the room is empty. Mid-morning. People are busy with chores and shopping.

Except for Fiza Farooq, curled up on one of the battered sofas. It's odd to see her without her mother: as if half of her is missing. Knees drawn up under her, she has a book on her lap. She glances up and smiles.

'Back from running?' she says.

I nod but I'm wary. She's been told so many times girls shouldn't run, she could probably repeat her mother's lectures word for word. I'm not about to give her that chance.

'It's a good day for running,' Fiza says.

I'm a little surprised she's not frowning and tutting.

'It's a great day,' I say.

Talking to Fiza is like talking to a smaller, quieter version of her mother – they're a mirror of each other, except Fiza rarely speaks. She listens and nods and smiles, but hardly says anything. I realise I don't actually know what goes on in her head. Now, she glances down at her book and up at me again. Is she waiting for me to start a conversation? She's still in primary school so although she travels into town in the bus every morning, we don't see each other in school. In the Centre, she's either trotting on her mother's heels or curled up somewhere with books.

'Doing schoolwork?' I ask.

Fiza nods. She must be top of her class by now. Not like me. I think of the book club and a little seed of an idea comes into my head.

'You like reading, don't you?' I say to Fiza.

She nods again, stronger this time.

'I've been asked to join a book club,' I say cautiously. She looks at me, interested. 'Do you know how they work? What they do?'

Fiza's face lights up as she explains all about book clubs.

'They usually have a topic or a theme,' she says. She's lively and animated as she talks, more than I've seen her before. 'Maybe books that have been made into movies, or books about travel. Does your book club have a theme?'

'I'm not in a book club!' I say. Even the thought scares me at the moment. 'They read books about other countries.'

Fiza nods. 'Books are only part of what book clubs are about, Azari.' She reminds me of Sharnaz explaining something to me. 'It's mostly about *talking* about books and having opinions on the story and the characters, and then chatting with other people.'

'But you have to read the books?'

'Of course.' She gives a little laugh. 'You do that outside of the club, though. Between meetings.' She smiles shyly at me. 'If you want, I could help you read the books?'

'Would you really? That would be great.' I smile at her. 'You study a lot – I'm not so good at schoolwork or reading.'

Fiza sits up a little. She peers behind me. I turn, expecting her mother at my shoulder, but nobody's there.

'Mother *thinks* I study more than I do.' Her voice is little more than a whisper.

'Are you not studying right now?' I'm curious.

Fiza lifts the book. Nestled in her lap is a mobile phone.

'Where did you get that?' I ask. 'Is it your father's?'

Perhaps obedient little Fiza isn't quite what she seems. She shakes her head.

'Father bought it to help with my homework.' She smiles. 'I use it to message friends and look at videos.'

I stare at the phone. So many questions run through my head. A good obedient Orthodox girl – conservative little Fiza – using a phone to message friends instead of studying? This is big news. At home, only men have mobile phones. Most women in my village don't read or write, and kids never have phones. But here's Fiza, still in primary school, with her own phone, messaging her friends. Her *friends*. Looking up videos. *Lying* to her mother. How did she get to be so Irish so quickly?

Phones aren't allowed in school, but everyone is on them before and after school: Irish girls, girls in Black School, tall brown boys hanging around for the bus. Everyone is cool and Irish, stuck on their phones except me. If I had a phone,

I'd be like everyone else. I'd be more Irish. I'd have friends. Friends like Emer, who I've seen a few times in school. She's always friendly, always smiles. We greet each other on the corridor and I wish I was in the same class as her so we could talk about stuff.

Now, I perch on the arm of the sofa next to Fiza. She's eager to show me more.

'It's new, so I'm still learning. I thought I'd only use it to look up English words and maths, but there's much more. A website about my home town.' She gives me a little sideways smile. 'And running clubs in Ireland, if you're interested.'

I'm more than a little curious now. I gaze at images on the little screen: teenagers in running bibs, holding medals and smiling. I'm itching to ask more but say nothing for now. My head is spinning. I'm still figuring out this new information about Fiza. Still wondering if I trust her.

'I message our family back home to tell them how we're getting on,' Fiza says. 'My friend tells me what's going on in our town.'

'Your friend at home has a phone?' I find this hard to believe: Sharnaz and I didn't know anyone our age with a phone. Girls aren't trusted to use them.

Fiza shakes her head. 'An older brother of a friend of mine. He's working in the city.'

Fiza is messaging an older boy? Her mother would have a fit if she knew. 'Who pays for it all?'

'Free wi-fi in the library. Other places too,' she says. 'I never use my data. Father says it's too expensive.'

This means nothing to me – it's like a second new language to learn after English: phone-talk.

Fiza smiles. 'I'll show you in the library if you like. Look up your village if you want? There might be a website run by the village council.'

Look up my village? The village council? I stare at Fiza. An icy sweat breaks out on my back. As though in slow motion, my two separate lives – Ireland and my home village – crash violently together, exploding in my head. My heart pounds. Fear clenches my stomach: Father is only a website away, in Fiza's hand? Close enough to reach me.

I stand up. Back towards the door.

'I'll think about it.' My words come out in a whispered croak. 'I need to shower.'

I can't talk about this right now. I can't even *think* about this right now.

I turn and run up the stairs, panic thundering in my head.

· · ·

'I don't see why we must spend all day doing this,' Mother says. 'Two buses there, two buses home. Hours of walking. We'd be safer staying in the Centre.'

'I'm not allowed go on my own,' I tell her for the umpteenth time.

'I'm sure there's legal aid closer than this.' She turns to me. 'Have you even looked?'

Mother has been grumbling since we left the Centre early this morning. It took all my powers of persuasion to get her to come with me. It's her fear and her broken heart that make her grumpy and stop her doing things. She'll have pains in her bones and will take to the bed after today, but we've no choice.

'There's no way around it, Azari,' Sheila said when I spoke with her by phone. 'Even though you're the one doing the work anyway, I have to swear all meetings with you were in the presence of an adult. And your mother will have to make her mark on the papers.'

Mother is in a right mood when we finally get to the legal offices. She won't speak to me or Sheila. She crosses her arms and stares out the window. It's embarrassing.

Sheila comments on my English straight away. 'You're almost fluent. And your accent already sounds Irish.'

'I've very much to learn yet. My writing is bad.' I blush, but inside, I'm proud. 'We have extra classes in school. They help, though I had to miss a whole day today to come here.'

'I'm delighted you're back in school,' Sheila says. 'Even though your English is so good, we'll use an interpreter today. These questions are difficult and it's important you – and your mother –' she glances at Mother's back and winks at me, 'understand what you're signing. These are the documents the IPO will use to decide whether you can stay in Ireland.'

Once the interpreter is on the phone, Sheila goes through pages and pages of the questionnaire. We check over our replies. Agree the documents and evidence to support our application. My written story from my first interview is to be included. I sign everything and then ask Mother to mark X on the pages.

'You do it for me,' she says, rubbing her legs. 'My old fingers can't hold the pen.'

Mother is ashamed when others see she can't write, but Sheila won't let me do it for her. 'She must make her own mark,' she says. 'It's the law.'

Reluctantly, Mother scores X on the page under my signature. Sheila gives me a copy of the documents before packing everything into an envelope.

'Once this goes in, you'll receive a reply and a document to prove you've made the application. Keep them safely.'

'What happens then?' I ask.

'You'll be assigned a case-worker to arrange a personal interview with you. Could take months – probably after the summer. So get on with your lives as best you can. You'll need legal aid before the interview to help you prepare and to attend with you on the day.'

'Can you do it with us?'

Sheila shakes her head. 'I can only help with the questionnaire. Someone else will help you for the interview. It'll be difficult, Azari. Other refugees have said the interviews are upsetting. You'll fret before, and worry afterwards too. I'll give you names of organisations to help you, and somewhere closer to your Centre so it's easier to meet them.' She smiles. 'Then you won't have to miss a whole day of school.'

I'm sad Sheila can't help us any more. I like her and am comfortable talking to her.

'You can ask for another woman solicitor,' she says. 'And for a woman to interview you in the IPO if you prefer. I know that's easier for you. Keep in touch with me. Let me know how things go and if I can help.'

We thank Sheila and say goodbye. It feels I'm closing another part of our life, moving on again. We're being cut loose and set adrift. It makes me nervous.

.   .   .

We're hungry as we leave the legal aid office. It's been a long time since cereal and bread before eight this morning.

'What I would give for pakora or flatbread,' Mother says.

She's more like herself now the formal part of the day is over. She's no longer anxious. As we walk to the bus, I glimpse our national flag above a small restaurant down a side road.

'We have a little money, Mother. How would you like a treat of traditional food?'

As soon as we open the door, the aromas transport me home. My heart swells with the fragrant spices and rich savoury smells. Mother squeezes my arm, her eyes lighting up.

The owner is from our home country, but up north. A different province. He welcomes us warmly. 'New arrivals in Ireland? We're truly honoured you're visiting us. Everything from home is still deep in our hearts, although we're living in Ireland almost twenty years.'

He shows us to a table with a white cloth and silver cutlery. I thought we might get a cheap takeaway. Now I'm worried this is an expensive restaurant we can't afford. This wasn't such a good idea.

'I have been changing our traditional recipes to suit the Irish palate for so long,' the owner confides in us. 'It would be an honour to prepare real home food for you, using only the best spices and fresh chillies.'

Dishes start arriving to the table. Now I *know* this is an expensive restaurant we can't afford. We haven't even been shown a menu. I don't know how much anything costs.

'We can't pay for all this food, Mother,' I whisper.

But she isn't interested in money. It means nothing to her. The owner's wife has come out from the kitchen and she and the owner join us at the table. Mother is much more interested in comparing recipes and spices. In discussing the differences between dishes from their province and ours. They tell us about arriving in Ireland twenty years ago. Mother tells them of our application process, although she doesn't go into detail about why or how we came here.

I let them talk while I enjoy the dishes. The food is wonderful. It's been almost a year since I last tasted traditional food. With every mouthful, memories of home flood back, filling me with strong emotions and a great longing for my country. When we've eaten everything we can, there's still so much food on the table.

'We'll wrap it up for you,' the owner says. 'To enjoy later.'

While they carry the dishes away, I turn to Mother. 'How are we going to pay for all this? We don't have so much money.'

'It's OK, little one,' she says. 'Wait and see.'

The owner and his wife return with paper bags of food cartons.

'It means so much to us to share food with you today. Come again.' They hand over the bags. 'Accept these as a gift from us. It was an honour to host you.'

'You knew they weren't going to charge us, didn't you?' I say to Mother later as we board our bus.

She gives a little smile. 'When they didn't ask what dishes we wanted, and then they joined us for food, we were dining as their friends and not as their customers. They are good people. We were fortunate to find their restaurant.'

It's dark and late when we finally trudge up the driveway to the Centre. Mother and I are exhausted.

'You missed dinner,' the manager says.

But I don't care. I'm so full of real food, I don't think I'll eat for a week.

Chapter 8

In the days following Sharnaz's disappearance, Mother and I were outcasts in our village, shunned by the people we had lived among all our lives. Villagers shut doors in our faces or turned their backs when we walked down the street. Stones flung by unseen hands stung me as I hurried to the bus before dawn. Mother was spat at in the street.

Home was more dangerous by far. Father was unpredictable and explosive, unleashing his fury at the slightest provocation. Anything set him off – the boys' laughter. The eggs overcooked. His tea too hot. He erupted, striking whoever he could reach before we fled. Dishes were overturned and smashed, food scattered on the floor. Not even Kashif and Musa were safe. No longer recognising the kind man who brought them fishing or played cricket with them, the boys took to eyeing him from the doorway before daring to enter the house. They were used to his clenched fist, but not this. None of us was used to this.

He didn't speak to Mother and me other than to tell us the Sharifs were demanding justice.

'You will pay heavily for your actions,' he said. 'For hiding her.'

The village council planned to discuss the scandal and agree penalties against Father for the money the Sharifs had paid for wedding gifts and preparations, and for their shame and loss of face in the community. There was also Uncle Rashid's original debt for the cow, yet to be settled. Uncle Rashid and Father were excluded from deliberations and would only be told the outcome.

'What are your ghosts telling you?' I asked Mother so often, she was sick of it.

'Nothing good,' was all she would say, but more than once, I caught her looking at me from under her lashes, her expression distracted and worried.

'Is it about me?' I asked.

She wouldn't say.

I fretted for Sharnaz, who seemed to have vanished from the earth. Her absence broke my heart in a million pieces and stole my sleep and appetite. Where was she hiding? Where had she gone? No friend, no family member would dare shelter her. No-one would dare to cross Father and the Sharifs.

The men of the village hunted her like prey, led by my father. They upended every home and outhouse in the village and further beyond, pitched out stores and barns and outhouses, scoured fields. Father even burned our own small field, scorching it to stubble in case Sharnaz had thought to hide among the tall leafy plants. We watched orange flames engulf the green corn and tomatoes. The odour of thick smoke clotted the air and blotted the colours from the sun. The washing hanging over the mulberry bushes was stained yellow and had to be washed again. When the fire burnt itself out, charred spikes stood twisted and crumbling into the ruined earth, blackening our hearts and sickening our thoughts.

Days dragged by and no sign of Sharnaz. Was she sleeping on the streets? At the side of the road? When the sun set each evening and darkness covered the village, I lay on the charpoy and prayed for her. I wondered where she was laying her head. I dreaded what would happen if they found her.

Two days after what should have been the wedding ceremony, a great commotion erupted on the laneway outside our house. Shouting and kerfuffle and uproar. Mother ran with me and the boys to see what was happening.

An untidy crowd of villagers scuffled and tussled on the street outside. At first, I thought it was a fight between gangs of boys, then I saw four men in front leading the unruly crowd towards our house. Father was among them, his white *shalwar kameez* dirt-streaked and stained. It was difficult to see clearly what was happening: dust rose from the street, kicked into the hot air. The sun shone in my face, dazzling me.

The men dragged and pulled something hanging between them. Stragglers yelled and screeched, sometimes darting closer to kick or strike at the small thing twisting and turning. Sticks swung in the air, mixing with the shouts of the rowdy angry crowd. The throng boiled with frenzy. Women and girls followed at the back, scarves over their heads. I glimpsed Deeba among them, her mouth wide, her face twisted in an ugly shout as she fired clods of dirt and earth, screaming and spitting and cursing the bloody thing. Small children ran alongside, hurling pebbles and shouting. My own brothers, excited by the sight and caught up in the emotion, ran to join the crowd, but I was quicker. I grabbed them as they burst past me and pitched them into the yard with a yell.

The men had found Sharnaz and were dragging her home.

I staggered back, folding my hands over my face. Beside me, Mother cried out.

They flung her on the dirt in our yard. She moaned a little, hardly moving. Breathless and jubilant, the men stood back. My beautiful sister was unkempt and filthy, her hair matted with blood, her dress ripped and tattered. No shoes or head-scarf on her, they had bound her tightly with ropes, her skin raw and bleeding. I hardly saw my sister beneath the bruises and swellings. Mother ran to her but was stopped by a shout from my father.

'This dog deserves no pity,' he said. 'It has brought shame and dishonour on this household and will pay for its sins.' He turned to me, his face twisted into a snarl that set my heart pounding. 'Let this be a lesson to you. You can't hide from your duty.'

I couldn't breathe. It was like something had stopped the air in my throat. I could only gasp and stare at Sharnaz. The sight of her tore at my heart, which beat so fast I thought it would burst through my ribs.

For the most part, the crowd didn't enter our yard, other than a handful of children and a couple of young men. Most people stood at the entrance to shout and curse my sister. To spit at my mother for raising a shameful daughter. To hurl stones. Deeba and her sisters were at the front of the throng, yelling and screaming. I ran to them, pleading.

'Why are you doing this? You were in school with us,' I cried. 'Sharnaz and I ran races with you! We played together as children.'

They shoved me back. Flung stones and insults. My voice was lost in the chaos.

While Father stood in the shade of the mango tree, sharing his chewing tobacco with Uncle Rashid, I crept to my sister's side, but there was little I could do while she lay in public view.

Now she had been dragged home, the crowd gradually dispersed. The afternoon's excitement over, mothers and fathers gathered up their children and wandered back to their homes. There was no sympathy for my sister nor any of the women of our house, only for my father, having to deal with the shame brought on him by his brazen daughter.

When the sun set and smoke from cooking fires and paraffin lamps drifted through the night, Uncle Rashid and Father finally walked to the market square with other men. Mother sent the boys to keep watch at the gate.

'Warn us if you see them,' she hissed.

Kashif and Musa were terrified, not only of Father but of the bloodied heap of rags they no longer recognised as their sister. They stood as told, looking anxiously at us as Mother and I ran to Sharnaz.

She had dragged herself to a dark corner at the side of the outhouse and was curled in a little heap in the dirt. I lifted strands of matted hair from her face so I could feed her drops of water. Her cracked lips moved when the water touched them, but no words came. We unknotted the rope. Sharnaz moaned as we prised it from deep grooves cut into her skin. One of her legs was swollen and unnaturally twisted. Her eye was horribly bruised and tightly shut. We washed dried blood from her face and hands, bandaged the worst of her wounds, covered her nakedness with a clean dress.

'He's coming,' Kashif hissed, tearing across the yard.

Mother took up the lamp and hustled them inside. I stayed next to Sharnaz.

'Azari?' Mother whispered.

'I'm not leaving her,' I said.

Sharnaz pushed her arm against me feebly, trying to make me go.

'I'm not leaving you,' I told her.

By the time Father came into the yard, Mother and the boys were safely in the house. I crouched in the darkness, but he never looked towards us. The door shut and we were alone.

The night deepened and settled itself around us in a blanket of comfort. I lay against the outhouse with Sharnaz in my lap, stroking her hair, murmuring to her. Every little while, I trickled drops of water onto her parched lips. I told her I loved her more than life itself, that I would protect her from harm. I swatted away the biting insects that came with the night, and the flies that would lay eggs in her wounds.

Sharnaz lay in my arms, mostly quiet, sometimes whimpering. I sensed her tension, her fear. Her bruised bones couldn't find comfort or ease. She moved her arms and legs constantly, trying to relieve her pain. Eventually she settled a little in my arms. Her breathing relaxed. Her stiffness eased. She slept at last. I rested my head and gazed at the million shining stars overhead. I tried to keep strong. I was there to protect and care for Sharnaz. Tears ran down my face for my sister.

I must've slept a little because I never heard Mother scuttling across the yard, a little light cupped in her hand. She knelt beside me, her breath uneven and trembling.

Her whisper made my blood run cold. 'They're going to kill her to restore family honour.'

My eyes flew open. I stared at Mother's shadowed face, unable to see her expression, struggling to understand what I had heard. I was careful not to tighten the hold I had on my sister: she was still asleep and mustn't know what was happening.

'Azari, do you hear me?' Mother said. 'It's planned for dawn. Father and Rashid are taking her from here.'

My body shook with fear like I had never known. 'We'll get her away to safety somewhere.'

'Where?'

I had no idea. Nobody in this village would help or protect us, but we had to do something.

'Aunt Hania's?' I said.

Mother shook her head. 'We can't.'

She was right. Their home had already been torn asunder over the last few days. Iman's father sided with my father and blamed Aunt Hania as much as Father blamed Mother and me.

I sat up a little, cradling Sharnaz in my arms. She woke immediately, crying out at the unexpected movement. She must've sensed my fear, for in an instant, she was rigid, her undamaged eye wide with terror, hands clasping at my shoulders.

'We're bringing you to safety, Sharnaz,' I whispered. 'We can't stay here.'

She hardly registered my words. I wasn't sure she even heard me. After her initial startle on waking, she became drowsy, dropping into my arms, head lolling against my chest. I murmured to her, shifted her gently to see if she could support herself.

'Hold her arms, Mother.'

We tried to get her to her feet, but she was unable to stand on her twisted leg, moaning with pain and sinking helplessly to the ground.

'We'll have to carry her,' I said.

We held Sharnaz in our arms and turned to leave the yard, but Mother froze. 'We'll be seen on the street.'

She was right.

'Through the field,' I said.

It was the only other way out of our yard.

We stumbled through the blackened twigs and thick ash of our scorched field, the burnt odour sharp in our nostrils. The ash softened our footfall, so we made no sound. Sharnaz hung in our arms, sometimes whimpering or gasping.

'The back tracks,' Mother said when we reached the far side.

The back tracks behind homes and streets, where food waste was flung in rotting heaps, rubbish was burned, places people used as open latrines, were usually avoided by villagers. They reeked of decay and human waste.

Flies buzzed around us, drawn by the heat of our bodies and the smell of blood. Moonlight gleamed on swarming rats; it was impossible not to step on them. More than once, a soft body wriggled from under my feet, setting my skin crawling.

'Stop for a little break,' Mother said once we cleared the back tracks and reached a narrow road. We were breathing hard.

'I don't think we've been seen,' I said.

We laid Sharnaz on the earth but couldn't stay long. Anyone could come along and the night must surely have turned over at this stage. Dawn might not be far off.

Sharnaz's breathing was unsteady and shallow. Blood seeped through her bandages.

'We'll take her to the sacred pool,' I said. 'We won't be seen there.'

'Then what?' Mother's eyes shone in the moonlight.

I didn't know. There was nowhere we could go that would be safe. I couldn't bring myself to tell Mother the dread in my heart as we hoisted my sister into our arms again. Sharnaz barely whimpered now, as though she was no longer aware of her surroundings. This made me more certain of what I believed: my beloved sister was slipping farther from us with every heartbeat.

Slowly and carefully, we picked our way down the path, each of us wrapped up in our own private thoughts. I stepped through the grass and mud, soon hearing the gurgle and splutter of the river. The air stirred where the water tumbled into a shallow pool overhung with night jasmine. The breeze was softly scented by the hundreds of tiny white flowers studded among the dark vines. Sharnaz used to call them fallen stars.

We laid her on the mossy bank.

Beyond where we stood, the little river widened and deepened to the dark pond where fish swam. A holy pool, overlooked by a shrine to a local goddess. The water was pure. Sacred. Children never swam here. Candles always burned at the feet of the little stone statue. Perfumed smoke from incense sticks curled through the air.

I wanted to bless Sharnaz in the holy waters. To cleanse her of the shame and fear clinging to her from the day Father had promised her to Abbas Sharif. I wanted her to be pure and renewed.

I stepped down first, cool water creeping up my calves, my thighs. 'Help me lift her.'

Together, we eased Sharnaz into the water, as gently as possible. She twitched a little, cried out. Then she was silent and still, floating, supported in my arms. The water calmed her. Her limbs relaxed a little. I trickled holy water over her head and murmured a prayer. Mother stepped in beside me. We blessed her. Prayed together. Her eyes were closed, her breath came in little gasps. She lay against me, nestled close to my heart. She looked beautiful.

Sharnaz stopped breathing. I looked into her face. Called her name. After a moment, she inhaled sharply. Arched her back. Her eyelids flickered. I looked at Mother, then back at Sharnaz. I listened to her breathing, touched her face with my fingertips.

'Don't do that, Sharnaz,' I whispered to her. 'You're scaring me half to death.'

I could see her face a little more clearly now: night was almost over. The black of the star-studded sky was fading to grey.

'Dawn is coming,' Mother said. 'We're not far enough away.'

'She can't go any farther.'

As though she heard me, Sharnaz stopped breathing again.

'Sharnaz! Sharnaz!' I held her tightly, willed her to breathe. 'Don't leave me. Please stay. Breathe.'

And she did, tiny shallow breaths that eased my heart even though it was breaking. We wouldn't have my sister for much longer. Even if she lived through tonight, what faced her at home? What faced any of us at home?

'She'll be safe here,' I said, stroking her cheek with my fingers. 'The goddess will take care of her.'

My tears mingled with the river water.

Dawn was flooding the sky now: pink and gold seeped into the clouds. The dying night promised a blessed dawn. I cradled my dying sister as gently as I would cradle an infant. She was slipping away as fast as the night. I looked at her beautiful, damaged face. Her eyelashes fluttered on bruised cheeks. She was so fragile, so beautiful. I loved her so much.

Across the mirrored surface of the sacred pool, masses of water lilies floated, single fat buds sitting on each pad. Pure white at their tips, the buds blushed to palest pink, then deep pink at their bases.

'I'll bring her closer to the shrine,' I whispered. 'Where they won't find her.'

Mother hugged and kissed Sharnaz. Stroked her face. She whispered her love and blessed her first daughter. Sharnaz was unaware of us, hardly drawing breath. Slowly, I walked with her in my arms through the sacred pool. My feet sank in the mud, the water at my waist now. Each time Sharnaz stopped breathing, it lasted longer, and when she stirred again, it was slower, less certain. Her time had almost come.

The water lilies under the darkness of the trees were tightly closed. As the air brightened and colour soaked into the morning, they would open, layer upon layer of petals to reveal their golden hearts. Night insects had already vanished. Sleepy dragonflies appeared, shimmering green metal, their glassy wings fluttering.

When my sister stopped breathing for the last time, my heart broke. I waited and waited, willing her to stir again, but there was nothing.

'Please, Sharnaz,' I said. 'Breathe.'

She didn't stir.

I looked back at Mother, standing in the shallows. And when she heard my sobs, she knew.

It seemed I would for ever be like the flower of a water lily, holding Sharnaz in my heart, safe and protected within a thousand folded petals. Nothing, *nothing* – not my father, not the promise of marriage, not my village – was going to harm her again. I kissed her and whispered my love to her. I released her to the water lilies. To the goddess, who was watching over us. Sharnaz floated among the flowers, pale and still. The green water closed over her beautiful face and she sank into the depths.

.   .   .

The world was coming to life. Early morning streets were bright and busy. Chickens pecked and scratched and fluffed feathers in the dust. A woman drove her goats along the road, staring at us as she passed. School children ran by. Two men on scooters piled high with fresh fruit and vegetables buzzed past. One of them spat in our direction. I didn't care.

Such life and activity felt wrong. Out of place. I was numb inside, my heart hollowed out. I would never see my sister again, yet all around me, the world was waking to a new day. An ordinary day. A day torn apart. Nobody knew my world had stopped. I didn't care for any of them.

All I could think was I wouldn't see my Sharnaz again.

I was an outsider, looking at life, but completely separate from it. My life had stopped. My world was over. It was as though I had stepped off and it was spinning on without me. I couldn't imagine ever getting back on again. What had played out in the sacred pool this dawn made this a day burned into my soul for ever.

'What now?' Mother said, her words scarcely more than a

whisper. Wet clothes clung to her body; her face was streaked with tears and ash. She looked exhausted. At that moment, she wasn't only talking about home. She was talking about our lives, our world. *What now?* I knew exactly what she meant.

Ahead of us was the spreading tree and half a dozen women waiting for the bus to town. I knew most of them. They stared at Mother and me. One or two recognised us, their eyes hostile, accusing. Others were probably shocked by our appearance: unkempt and soaked. I looked away as the bus trundled up. The women crowded on, chattering and distracted. No longer interested in us.

Without thinking, I grabbed Mother's hand. Pulled her on the bus with me. And she came. Neither of us said a word; the women ignored us. We crouched in the corner, dripping a little puddle of pond water as the bus carried us from our home and village. Away from where Sharnaz lay at peace beneath the water lilies.

Everyone poured off the bus in town and disappeared into the streets. We stood, uncertain what to do, where to go. A shout startled me.

'Azari!'

Komal ran up, a scarf held over her face. She hugged me, nodded to Mother when I introduced her. 'We're all set up. Let's go!'

I stared at her. Numb. Confused. 'Where?'

Komal wasn't listening. She looked behind me. 'Where is she?'

'Who?' I was confused.

Komal stopped. Her eyes searched my face. 'Sharnaz – is she with you?'

I didn't know how to reply. My eyes filled with tears as my heart broke all over again. I watched the understanding dawning in Komal's eyes.

'She's gone, Komal. We couldn't do anything.'

'No!' she cried out. 'No, Azari! She was so close. She was going to get away. We had it all worked out. We had a *plan*. What happened?'

'Father found her,' I said. 'Dragged her home.'

'Sharnaz was with you?' Mother's voice was soft. 'All the time, she was here?'

'Not with me, but in Panah. She was safe there.' She took Mother's hands. 'I'm sorry for worrying you, but it had to be a secret. It was the only way she could be safe. We cared for her until we had everything ready.'

I stared at her, confused. 'You knew where she was all this time, and you wouldn't tell me? Even when I asked?'

'Sharnaz forbade me,' Komal said. 'She wanted you to be safe. It meant everything to her.'

'What is this Panah?' Mother asked. 'Is it the factory?'

'A shelter,' Komal said. 'A safe place for women and girls in danger. I brought Sharnaz there when …' She glanced at me. 'When her ribs were broken. Panah made arrangements for her to leave town.'

'How did Father find her?' I said. 'If she was so safe, how was she found?'

'She wanted to go back to the village. It was her decision.' Komal's words broke with a sob.

'She knew what Father was like,' I said. 'Why would she come back when she was safe here?'

'To get you, Azari,' Komal said. 'She wouldn't leave without you. She wanted you with her.'

I stared at Komal, hardly believing her words. 'Me?'

'She wanted you to be free to run,' Komal said. 'She knew how much it meant to you.'

'Where were we supposed to be going?' I asked.

'Where no-one would find you,' Komal said. 'Where you'd both be safe. She got the bus back to fetch you and to say goodbye to your mother. We tried to stop her but she was determined. "One day, Komal," she said. "I only need one day."'

'Sharnaz had no money. No papers,' Mother said. 'How could she get away?'

'Panah has helped many girls,' Komal said. 'Makes arrangements, pays the costs. I work for Panah. Help women in the factory.'

'Where would be safe from Father?' I asked.

'A long way from here,' Komal said. 'I've been waiting here all night. We were to meet before dark.' Her eyes filled with tears again. 'I hid behind the bins, watched every bus. When I saw you this morning, I thought she had got away. That you were both safe.' She shook her head. Stopped speaking.

We stood together, holding hands. So many thoughts spun in my head. So much was happening. Our dreams had been close to coming true. We were close to being happy and free.

'It's not too late for you,' Komal said. 'They're waiting for us at Panah. We've all the arrangements made for two of you.'

Mother and I stood unmoving, unsure what to do.

'You can't go home, Azari.' Komal looked at me. 'Your father will beat you both, perhaps kill you.'

'Nasir is my husband,' Mother whispered. 'I'm bonded to him. I can't leave.'

'He killed Sharnaz, Mother. He'll kill us too.' My words shocked me. They shocked my mother.

'But the boys …' she began.

'They'll be fine,' Komal said. 'Boys always are. Come to Panah for now. We'll decide after that.'

.   .   .

A few rooms on the ground floor of our garment factory, under the concrete steps I had climbed a thousand times. Offices where women worked on phones and computers. A little kitchen.

Komal directed us to sit on plastic chairs. 'Give me five minutes.'

A curtain hung over a doorway behind the office, and through the gaps, I glimpsed three women on narrow charpoys. Perhaps Sharnaz had slept in there, safe and secure while Father hunted her down. How I wished she had stayed here and not come back for me.

'We have to go home, Azari.' Mother tugged at my sleeve. 'We should never have come on the bus. What were we thinking?'

'Wait, Mother,' I said.

'Your father doesn't know about Sharnaz. Now we're gone too.' She stood up, pulled me towards the door.

I was confused. Exhausted. Frightened. 'Maybe something good can come of this.'

'Nothing good will come from disobeying Nasir. It will only anger him further.' Mother moved away from me. As she turned, she almost collided with a woman holding two cups of fresh water.

'I brought these for you.' The woman smiled. 'I'm Yalina. Please, rest a moment.'

Mother was uncertain. Shy with this woman's kindness.

'This is difficult for you,' Yalina said. 'Come inside and talk. You must be exhausted.'

She was gentle. Before we knew what was happening, we were in a smaller office, sitting with Komal and Yalina. Yalina's smooth hands and polished nails, her office clothes, glossy hair: everything about her was different from us. I hid my rough hands in my lap, with their broken nails and scuffed knuckles. My clothes were mud-streaked and reeked of pond water.

'I am devastated to hear of Sharnaz's death,' Yalina said. 'Komal told me. It must be heartbreaking for you.'

I nodded, but didn't trust myself to speak. Mother said nothing.

'She had such a bright future. So many dreams. So many hopes. But you, Azari.' My heart skipped when she addressed me directly. 'You still have that bright future. You have so much promise. So much potential. The next Jinani Azad, I hear?'

I stared at her. Had Sharnaz spoken about me?

'You must be confused,' Yalina said. 'We would like to help you.'

'Azari's first duty is to her father,' Mother said. 'Mine is to my husband. Thank you for helping my first daughter, but we must leave.'

'Is that what you want?' asked Yalina. 'To return to a man who beats you? Who killed your daughter? Who will probably marry off Azari in the same arrangement?'

I gasped.

'People like us don't have choices,' Mother said. 'We're not rich. We have nowhere to go. We'd be on the streets.'

'When my husband attacked me, I was helped by someone who told me there are always choices,' Yalina said. 'Always places to go.'

I wondered how such a powerful woman could ever have been attacked.

'I was also married off when I was fifteen to a man four times my age,' Yalina said. 'As his second wife, I slaved in his fields from dawn to dusk. Cooked for him and his grown children. When I couldn't give him sons, he dragged me into a field, threw acid on me and left me for dead.'

She unwound her shimmering scarf, lifted glossy hair. There was no hair on the left side of her scalp. Instead, the skin was red and shiny, melting down her face, her neck, disappearing under the collar of her dress. Her left ear was mostly gone, the skin knotted and mottled. Her eye too was badly damaged but the scars were cleverly concealed with make-up.

'After months of treatment, I recovered. A woman doctor helped me get away from my husband. There are always choices – if only we are strong enough to change.'

I breathed deeply, unaware I had been holding my breath.

'I made a new life for myself,' Yalina said. 'I started Panah to help girls and women. We are funded by the government and international aid. We've volunteers and workers in garment factories all over town. Panah has helped dozens of women escape their abusive husbands and fathers.' She turned to Mother. 'People like you do have choices.'

Yalina tied up her scarf again. Rearranged her hair so her scarring was hardly noticeable. 'Sharnaz wanted you to have a better life, Azari. Don't waste her sacrifice.'

I had already made my decision. 'I'm not going home.'

'Azari?' Mother spun to me.

'What's there for me, Mother? Sharnaz is gone. I work all hours in the factory for nothing. Father will want to marry me to Abbas Sharif. But look! Here's something else. Here, I might have a future.'

'You must do your father's duty,' Mother said.

'Azari must choose her own future,' Yalina said.

'I want to do what Sharnaz wanted for me, Mother,' I said. 'She gave her life for me.'

'And what about me?' Mother whispered. 'What will I do?'

'Come with me.'

Chapter 9

On the day of the book club, I hover outside the school library at lunchtime. I'm nervous and uncertain. Is this what I want to do?

Before I have a chance to change my mind, the door bursts open and Emer is there, dragging me in and introducing me to a dozen other girls. The school librarian is there too, and she smiles and gestures for me to sit down. I've never been in the school library before. As we settle on beanbags and soft armchairs, I look around at the shelves of books, the colourful posters, the comfy seating. It's a welcoming place.

To begin with, everyone chatters and talks and laughs. Once the conversation settles down, the librarian welcomes me and then explains we're first going to talk about the book everyone read last month. She holds up the book and a discussion on the story starts. The conversation is noisy and unruly, and it's interesting to listen as everyone gives her opinion: what they liked or didn't like, what worked and what didn't. The librarian asks unusual questions to get everyone thinking. There's talk about the country where the book is set and what everyone learned about its food and customs.

Then we decide what to read next. The librarian has some suggestions. So do a few of the girls. They give a little summary of the books they've brought. With colourful covers and exciting stories, these books don't look or sound anything like schoolbooks. They're set in different countries from all parts of the world and everyone gets to vote – including me. I surprise myself by voting to read a book about a family from Syria who have to flee their home to get away from a war tearing their country apart. I want to find out if their experience is anything like mine. And it turns out to be the book that gets most votes, which I'm a bit excited about. Imagine me voting to read a book in English – Sharnaz will be astonished when I tell her.

'So you're coming to the next meeting?' Emer asks as we leave the library.

I shrug and smile. 'Maybe.'

'Welcome to the book club.'

It seems that I'm now a member. I'll definitely need Fiza to help me.

．　　　．　　　．

When I get back to the Centre, new signs are all over the place, laminated and printed in bold red letters:

·　NO MEETINGS WITHOUT MANAGEMENT
　　PERMISSION

- PRIVATE MEETINGS NOT PERMITTED
- TV ROOM FOR ALL RESIDENTS

Somebody has written 'Police State' above the notice. And 'Free speech' instead of 'Private meetings.' And 'Detainees' in place of 'Residents.'

Talk over the Saturday burger dinner is all about Princess's meeting. What it was about. When there's another one. I never heard so many women talking about one thing. The canteen is excited and energetic. There's talk of traditional meals and favourite foods. Men are interested too: foods they loved to buy or grow or eat. The busy markets they worked in before a war blew them up. The spices they ground before they became homeless. The street foods they fried before they ran in fear of their lives. Arguments about age-old recipes, spices, the best side-dishes. The meeting has started a blizzard of talking and sharing.

Princess comes over to our table. 'I've been given a warning.'

'What kind of warning?' I ask.

'Try a *trick* like that again and they'll have me *moved*.'

'Can they do that?'

'Not without a fight on their hands. I'll report them for denial of my right to speech. I've done *nothing* wrong.'

'What's going to happen now?' I drop my voice. 'Are we meeting again?'

'The yard after dinner.' She winks at us. 'If you're brave enough.'

I'm not sure about the Farooqs, but Mother wants to attend.

'Queenie is right,' she says, her eyes bright.

'Queenie? Her name is Princess, Mother.' I say.

'How can we survive without traditional dishes?' Mother says to me and the Farooqs. 'How will you run your home without proper foods? No self-respecting husband will accept greasy Irish dishes with unnatural colours!'

Princess is clever to arrange her next meeting in the yard: nobody can throw us out. Although it's dark, it's not wet or cold. The electric light from the prefab shines on a score or more women and girls who gather, and a few random others waiting for the washing machines, bags of laundry at their feet. Princess stands on the step to the prefab.

Mother pokes me in the ribs. 'Tell her about green mangoes.'

'Wait until she starts,' I say.

Princess clears her throat. Everyone falls silent. 'How will our sons and daughters know traditional foods if we can't cook our dishes?' says Princess, as though she's already heard Mother's words. 'They must cook and eat meals with ingredients from our homelands. We need flavours of our childhood to heal the homesickness and the heartsickness.'

I translate for Mother. Her eyes close. She draws deep breath as though homesickness and heartsickness hurt her physically.

'You mad!' says a familiar voice behind Princess.

Meri stomps out of the prefab, a fat bundle of clothing clutched in her arms. I half-expect her to whip out a packet of crackers and start munching.

'You mad,' Meri says again to Princess. 'How we can cook in this place? It all rules, rules, rules. No kitchen. No fridge. No ingredients. We are money-makers for manager. Nowhere to make blood dumplings. Beetroot pancakes. Boiled trotters.'

'Thank God for that,' someone shouts.

Women laugh but Meri is serious and upset. Her eyes are bright with tears. Her face is red. This is important to her.

'You're right, sister.' Princess reaches an arm around Meri. 'These are bad truths about this Centre, my friend. We are their business. Their monthly cheque. Nothing more.'

I'm startled Princess is agreeing when Meri called her mad, but Meri nods, satisfied. Princess has heard her. Princess has another sister by her side instead of a rival. She's smart, I think. She gets everyone to agree with her.

'We need to change things,' Princess says. 'We need to challenge these rules about no meeting, no free speech, no cooking. We are nothing, so we have to make ourselves *something*!'

'What is she saying?' Mother asks.

I translate as Princess continues. 'We must be allowed to cook for our health and happiness.'

'For survive,' says Meri.

'How?' one woman asks. 'Can't use kitchen. Can't use dining room. No money. No choice.'

'Can't store food,' someone else says.

There's murmuring and whispering. We're interested. We know it's important. But what to do next?

'Buy ingredients and share a meal,' Mother whispers to me. 'We can ask the manager.'

I don't know that I can speak Mother's idea out loud in front of everyone. Will they laugh at me? Get angry? My belly tightens up.

Mother pokes me. 'Tell her!'

Princess looks around at the faces. She catches my eye. I speak quietly. Make myself believe I'm only speaking to her. Nobody else. Only Princess.

'Collect money for food,' I say. 'Then maybe we cook a meal to share.'

Princess nods, smiles. She repeats it so everyone can hear.

'Where do we get ingredients?' someone says.

'What money?' says someone else.

'Who cooks?' asks a third.

Others mutter, talk, shake their heads. They're not certain, but nobody has other suggestions. There's discussion between everyone. People have a lot to say. We agree to give a little money every week to buy ingredients. When we have enough money, a group of women will each cook one traditional dish from their country.

'A small collection from our allowance. Whatever you can manage,' Princess says. 'No contribution, no sharing the meal. When we have enough, we ask to use the kitchen for a few of us to cook.'

Women are nodding. Smiling. This is a good thing.

'Soul food,' Meri calls out, a big grin on her face.

'Soul food?' says Princess. 'What's soul food?'

'We are,' says Meri, gesturing to us all with a wide sweep of her arm. 'Altogether, we are *Soul Food*.'

And Princess gets what Meri means. She smiles. Nods.

'We need to call our cooking group something. Traditional dishes are part of who we are,' she says. 'Our hearts. Our bones. Our *souls*. Soul Food is a wonderful name.'

Mother is beside herself as we get ready for bed later. Her cheeks are flushed, her eyes bright. 'Do they sell goat meat in Ireland?'

'Are you thinking of Soul Food?'

'Maybe almond meatballs in tomatoes?'

'Oh, Mother, I already smell the spices!'

My mouth waters at the thought of one of my favourite dishes from home. Sharnaz and I used to help Mother to make it. And almond meatballs become another precious memory that has returned to me.

· · ·

Next day after school, Robert is in the library. He smiles when he sees me. We sit on the same chairs.

'You never told me where you seen me,' I say to him.

'When?'

'When you first talked to me. You said you seen me before but you never said where.'

'Out running,' he says. 'How else did I know you were a runner? It's not stamped on your forehead.'

I rub my forehead, confused for a moment until he laughs.

'A couple of Saturdays back, I seen you along the stretch of road out by the refugee centre,' he says. 'Am I right?'

The refugee centre. I'm immediately wary when he says that. People change when I tell them I live in Direct Provision.

Girls in my class look at me differently. The resource teacher thinks all refugees are friends. The PE teacher feels sorry for me. I like Robert. I don't want him to change what he thinks of me because of where I must live.

His words cut across my thinking.

'It's not a trick question or nothing,' he says. 'It was you, wasn't it? Or have you a twin?'

'I don't have a twin.' I smile. 'It was me.'

He doesn't miss a beat. 'You were eating up the road when I seen you. Some pace you set yourself.'

'Where were you?'

'In my da's car heading to a match,' he says. 'Would you be up for a long run some weekend?'

He says it so naturally, I'm not even sure I've heard him right. 'With you?'

'No, on your own. Like you're already doing.' He laughs. 'Yeah – course with me. A real person to run with beats audiobooks or podcasts any day.'

For the second time, I hesitate. This is a bigger hesitation because it's a bigger question. I need to think this one through. I need to talk to Sharnaz. Princess. *Someone.* But Robert doesn't wait this time. He makes it easy for me.

'It's OK if you can't answer right off,' he says. 'I'm not asking you to rob a bank or nothing. It's only a long run, but maybe it's different for you. I know that. Just think it over, OK?'

'OK.'

My head is full to bursting as I get the bus back to the Centre that evening. Sharnaz has plenty to say on the matter.

No way, Azari. You've met him twice and now he wants to be on his own with you. That's suspicious. Definitely unsafe.

'We'll be running,' I tell her. 'He's not up to anything. It's in public.'

What would Mother say? And Father?

'I'm not about to tell Mother,' I say. 'And it would never happen with Father because I wouldn't be running at all.'

Don't make light of this! Running is the start of it. Next thing, he'll be asking you to meet him somewhere you can't be seen. That's when it's dangerous. He's softening you up, so you won't be suspicious.

'I don't think so, Sharnaz,' I say.

I'm only watching out for you, she whispers. *I've always been the wiser and more sensible one. You're useless: you don't see danger until it's too late.*

After dinner, Mother offers to help Mrs Farooq settle the two youngest children in bed. She's done that before, usually when she's been thinking about Musa and Kashif. It helps soothe her. Fiza and I are left together at the table. She leans across to me.

'Tomorrow after school in the library,' she says. 'I'll show you how my phone works. And we could look up running clubs.' She doesn't mention my village or the council.

'Great,' I say. 'Four thirty? I've also got a book for the book club. Will you help me with it?'

'We could try reading a little of it this evening, if you like?'

I see Princess a couple of tables away. 'Maybe tomorrow. I need to talk with Princess.'

I need a bit of advice on the Robert situation. I head over to Princess instead of leaving the canteen.

'Hey, Azari-Nike,' Princess pats the chair next to her, gesturing for me to sit down. 'Hey, Fiza.'

I spin around. To my surprise, Fiza is stuck right behind me, having followed me over. Same way she shadows her mother. Princess pulls out another chair for her, but I'm not so welcoming. What's Fiza following me for? I don't trust her, even if she is going to show me stuff on her phone. Last thing I want is Mrs Farooq hearing all about Robert and me, reporting it back to Mother and telling her how immoral I am by running alone with a white Irish boy. I'll never hear the end of how corrupt and shameless I am.

'Don't you have to help your mother?' I say to Fiza in our own language.

'Your mother is helping this evening.' She looks hurt.

'I'm sure she'll be wondering where you are.'

'I don't know what you two are talking about,' Princess laughs. 'I'm *good*, ladies, but I'm not *that* good. Let's switch to *English*.'

'It's OK,' Fiza says to Princess in English. 'I was on my way upstairs.'

'What was that about?' Princess says when Fiza's gone. 'I could have chopped the tension between you ladies with an axe.'

'She has to help her mother,' I say.

'Fiza looks up to you,' Princess says as I sit down. 'Let her into your heart a little. She's only young. Trying to find her place in this strange new world we're all in.'

'Looks up to me? I don't think so!' I'm surprised at Princess's words. 'Fiza's a mirror of her mother, who thinks *nothing* of me. Fiza learns everything from her mother. Sees me through her mother's eyes. Hears me with her mother's ears.'

'She's young. She doesn't have your worldly experience and maturity.' I glance sideways at Princess in time to see her wink. 'She's learning about her world. For some reason I can't fathom, she seems to be impressed by you. Don't cut her out, Azari-Nike.'

A smile twitches the corners of Princess's mouth.

'Her mother is always going to be critical of your rebellious nature, your strong spirit. She's scared for her daughter. Trying to protect her from wild Irish people. But Fiza is watching and taking it all in, even with her mother constantly whispering in her ear. She's growing up in Ireland now. Learning a whole lot of new stuff about how to behave. Give her a little time. I think we're going to see an independent personality blossom.'

'You think I have a rebellious nature?'

'It's written all over you.' Princess smiles. 'Am I wrong?'

'I left school and running when Father told me to,' I say. 'I started working in the factory as he said. I'm obedient. Do what my parents tell me. I'm not rebellious.'

'I believe you,' Princess says. 'But you don't have to be disobedient to be rebellious. You can rebel quietly. Obediently.'

I shake my head. Cross my arms. 'That's not me.'

'Look at you now – pushing right back against what I'm saying to you.' Princess settles back in her chair, a twinkle in her eye. 'Let me see. You're running – against your Father's wishes. You got out of your country! I imagine even leaving your village was against your father's wishes. You're pushing your mother towards residency in Ireland. That all sings to me of a rebellious nature. A strong spirit.'

I take in what she says, turn it over in my mind. Look at how the light slants on its angles and sides in new ways. Rebellious – is that me? Are my colours so different than I thought?

'Are you rebellious?' I ask.

'I think most people in Direct Provision are rebellious,' Princess says. 'We're here because we resisted control and authority in our home countries and our families. We didn't have a choice. We *rebelled*.'

'Maybe it's survival. Mother and I *had* to leave our home. We had to run for our lives from the village. The Farooqs *had* to leave theirs because their religion was being targeted. Other people are here to escape war or hunger.'

'Survival is a good word, my friend. Survival or rebellious – we all got away,' Princess replies. 'If we agreed with our senseless governments, obeyed the crazy rules, put up with war and hunger, we would still be in our home countries.'

'Or we might be dead!' I say.

'But we're not dead. Instead, we fought back. We rebelled. We survived. And we're here.'

'What did you rebel against in your country?' I ask her.

Princess sits back in her chair. Thinks for a bit. 'My type wasn't accepted in my country,' she says eventually. 'I had to decide to obey the crazy rules or be true to myself. I chose to be true to myself, Azari-Nike. But I might also be rebelling against the rules in Ireland.' For the first time, shadows of sadness darken Princess's words. It surprises me: she's always so positive, so driven to change for the better. Perhaps I don't know her as well as I think. 'I'm not sure where someone like me fits in.'

'You fit in with us here,' I say.

Princess hoots with laughter. It rings around the canteen. 'This Centre is no place to *fit in*; this is somewhere we all need to *get out* of.' She gets serious again. 'Sometimes people aren't always as they first appear. It's difficult for others to accept them. To understand them. We're all a bit afraid of difference. It makes life a struggle. But enough of me. What about you, Azari-Nike? What news have you of your new Irish friend?'

I tell Princess all about my conversation with Robert and my dilemma.

'What did Princess want to talk to you about?' Mother asks when I get back to the room later. 'Fiza said you stayed behind to talk with her.'

What? Fiza has already told Mother what I'm up to! I knew I couldn't trust her! Anything I say to her will get back to *her* mother, and from there, to *my* mother. Lesson learned for tonight. But Mother doesn't ask any more. She's all smiles. She strokes my arm, straightens the neckline of my dress.

'Was it good to help with the little ones? To tuck them up?' I ask her, thinking that's the source of her happiness.

'You're a good girl, Azari. You translate for me. You look out for me. You keep us safe.'

There's something else going on. I look at her closely. 'What are you up to?'

She tucks a loose strand of hair behind my ear. 'I was talking to Mrs Farooq.'

Putting more fears about Ireland into Mother's head, no doubt.

'Fiza has a phone,' Mother says.

'I know,' I say. 'She showed me.'

'To look up information,' Mother says.

And to message her friend's brother, play games, listen to music, I think. Not that Mrs Farooq knows any of her good daughter's activities.

'Would you use a phone?' Mother says.

'They're expensive.'

'You worry about your work-at-home.' She smiles. 'I've been saving money.' She looks happy and proud of herself. 'A little here. A little there.'

Does Mother have enough money saved to get us a little phone? One of the cheap supermarket ones? She doesn't know Irish money. She wasn't good with money at home because Father looked after it. Managing money is new for her. How much has she been hiding away?

'I got you a phone,' she says.

'*What?*'

This is *not* what I expected. My mother – who has hardly set foot outside the Centre since we got here – got a phone?

'How did you get a phone? *Where* did you get a phone?'

'A man helped me.'

Alarm bells ring inside me. 'What man?'

'The bus driver.'

'Seán? He got you a phone?'

'I paid him.'

'You gave *Seán* your money?'

This is not good. Seán is the meanest old git you ever met. I wouldn't trust him with anything.

Mother is a little less happy now. 'I asked Mr Farooq to do the business.'

'Mr Farooq?' This was getting worse. Mr Farooq is a lot like my father. 'You handed over your money to Seán and Mr Farooq?'

Mother's not listening any more. She's on her knees, reaching under the mattress.

'How much did you pay, Mother?'

She pulls out a paper bag.

'Did you get a receipt? Change? Is it even a new phone?'

I'm distracted by the bag. Trying not to get excited and rip it open. Seán and Mr Farooq could've taken any amount of money from Mother. She wouldn't know. She wouldn't question them. She would do what she has always done – let men make the decisions and do the business. I'm learning from Princess that women don't need to agree with men all the time. Women can make their own decisions. Mother hasn't learned this yet.

'Where did they get the phone, Mother?'

'Don't vex me,' Mother says. She's excited as she hands me the bag.

I tip it out on the bed, relieved to see the box is still sealed. It's new. Not some second-hand throwaway. A receipt flutters out too but Mother snatches it up.

'Look at your phone!' Her face is flushed with excitement.

I break the seal. Open the box. A sleek phone nestles inside. Pale pink. Shiny. Charger and earphones tucked beneath. It's perfect. My face is hot. My heart beats fast. I look at Mother, her face swimming through my tears of happiness.

'You got this for me?'

She strokes my face, she smiles. 'You need a phone to help you. Mrs Farooq says it makes learning better. Easier.'

I'm thinking of other things Fiza showed me. Messaging. Information about running. Games. Music. I unravel the cable, plug the phone into the wall socket. A little red dot lights up.

Mother smiles. 'Can we look up news from home?'

Every weekend back home, Father bought the local paper to read in the yard, sitting in the shade of the mango and chewing his tobacco. Occasionally he would share something that interested him: political elections in the next district or the result of a cricket match. When he discarded the paper, Sharnaz and I read to Mother the news that was much more interesting to her: births, deaths and marriages, village council decisions, ads for hair products and dress fabrics. She loved looking at the pictures and poring over the photographs. I smile at her.

'We can find out what's happening back home,' I say, even though the thought terrifies me. Suppose someone from our village finds out I'm looking up the council and tells Father? Suppose he reaches me through my new phone? I vow to only look up safe sites that have nothing to do with our village. But that's for another day. Right now, I can't stop thinking how much Seán might have charged Mother. Did he pocket her money? Does she even understand phone credit?

'You know there are charges for a phone,' I say to her.

'Mr Farooq told me. This is the cheapest package. Mr Farooq will do the credit every month and only charge a small price.'

'He wants to charge you to buy credit?' I can't believe this. I'm mad now. 'No, Mother. That's *our* money. It's not for Mr Farooq!'

I snatch up the receipt from the bed. 'Did they give you change?'

'Don't fuss,' Mother says. 'They were good to help me. They deserve a little payment for their trouble.'

So they both profited from Mother's trust! I'm furious.

I walk to the door. 'I'm going to get your money back.'

'No, no.' Mother's eyes open wide. She grabs my hand. 'Please, Azari. Don't cause trouble. I don't want to make them angry – you know how men can be.'

She's frightened. Father's temper, his outbursts, terrified her. Terrified us all.

'OK, OK.' I sit next to her. 'I won't do anything. They were good to help you, but it's not right for them to charge you.'

'But now you have a phone,' Mother says, smiling again. 'To help with your schoolwork.'

'And we won't be paying them anything to get credit. I'll do it myself.'

Chapter 10

'Why did you tell my mother I was talking to Princess?' I say to Fiza when we meet in the library. 'What business is it of yours?'

She looks at me, eyes wide with surprise.

'*Your* mother might need to know everything you're doing,' I say. 'But mine doesn't.'

Even as I'm saying the words, I think how Irish I sound. How I'm only saying it because I'm afraid Mother will find out about Robert. Because I have a secret. I never had a secret before. I never had something I couldn't tell Mother. I'm guilty and ashamed.

'I told her so she wouldn't go looking for you,' Fiza says.

'What?' This confuses me.

'She wanted to go down to the canteen to find you after my sisters were in bed,' Fiza says. 'But you wanted to talk to Princess in private, so I told your mother Princess needed to talk to you. Then she wouldn't interrupt you. She waited in your room for you instead.'

Maybe I was too quick to judge Fiza.

She goes on. 'Was that bad? I'm sorry for angering you. I would never tell your mother your business.'

'Thanks.' I'm gruff in my response. Fiza was helping me. That never occurred to me, but it still annoys me.

She leans closer. 'I would never even tell my mother *my* business.' She folds her arms. 'Or anybody else's business either.'

I smile at her, my irritation forgotten. Every time I speak with Fiza, I like her a little more. I should trust her more.

'Did you have your private talk with Princess?' she asks.

I nod, but I'm not about to share everything with her yet. 'Do you have time to read some of my book with me?'

For half an hour, Fiza helps me with the first couple of chapters. It's easier when she's there to help with the trickier parts. I pick up new words and remember them when I see them again. The story is exciting. We both gasp with shock when a bomb is thrown at two boys from a helicopter. We're eager to start the next chapter to see if they survive, but we also want to spend time looking at Fiza's phone. I'm also excited to show her my phone and to learn how to use it. We agree to get back to the book tomorrow.

Fiza is enthusiastic when I take my phone from the box. 'It's like mine!'

For the next while, she shows me the features on our phones and what she's set up on hers. We connect to the library wi-fi, exchange numbers, and she downloads apps and games for me. Apps. When she says the word, it reminds me of something.

'Emer said there's an app for the supermarket on the Wexford Road,' I say. 'Can you find it for me?'

I don't tell her why. Fiza's still only a child and doesn't yet need the free products this supermarket provides. She downloads the app in seconds. Reads some of the content.

'They do lots of weekly specials,' she says. 'I might get it for us too.'

I'm a little nervous she might also suggest we look up my village, but she doesn't mention it. She's too happy and distracted showing me other stuff. It's good chatting with her. She's smart and funny, and giggles in a way that reminds me of my little brothers.

'New phones?' says a familiar voice.

I lift my head. Robert stands next to us.

I'm thrown for a moment as my two separate worlds once again collide: the world of Direct Provision and Fiza and applying for refugee status, versus the world of white Irish boys and Ireland and running and being an ordinary teenager. I don't feel normal in either world, yet here I am in both. The moment smashes into me, like when Fiza offered to look up my village council on her phone: two worlds exploding in my head.

I'm lost for words. Don't know what to say. My heart pumps.

Robert makes it easy for me. Either he senses my discomfort

and knows to rescue me, or he's a natural at making someone feel at ease.

'Wait'll you see my phone,' he says, fishing a battered phone with a cracked screen from his pocket. He peers at it, frowning. 'Nothing as fancy as them ones for me. Think I've dropped this on almost every run. Don't know how it keeps going, but it's useful for podcasts and stuff. And it can just about send messages.'

Fiza too has an old head on her and can read stuff in a way I never could at her age. She's up on her feet in a flash, packing her bag, smiling and nodding at Robert. She says nothing but slips away like a little shadow. Gone. And for a fleeting moment of panic, I wonder if I was right to trust her. Is information about a white Irish boy about to make its way straight to the ears of Mrs Farooq?

Robert glances up. 'Did I scare her off?'

'She was leaving anyway.'

'Was it me phone that did it?' He shrugs. 'It's a bit of a scary monster, right enough.'

With Fiza gone, there's only one world to deal with. Everything slips back into place. I move into the world of the Irish teen. My heart slows down. It seems one world at a time is all I can handle.

'So, what's the story?' Robert asks.

I smile at him. 'Want to go for a run this Saturday?'

He grins at me. 'Deadly.'

.   .   .

'No cooking!' Princess shouts. 'No. Cooking. EVER!'

We're queuing up for cartons of chips and nuggets with red sauce when she strides into the canteen like a towering volcanic eruption, in a bright orange and red dress. Heads turn. People stop eating.

'No refugees in the kitchen!' Princess shouts. 'No foreign foods in the kitchen! No strange dishes in the kitchen!'

She presses her lips together tightly. Her forehead is creased. She's furious, but upset too, her eyes full of tears.

'Is she talking about Soul Food?' Mother asks.

'Think so,' I say.

'Nobody is allowed in the kitchen,' Princess shouts. 'Not once a month. Not once a year. Never!'

Her voice rises loud and high, singing above the clatter of trays and cutlery and voices. As she speaks, the clatter dies down. The voices stop. People turn to listen.

'The kitchen is out of bounds for refugees,' Princess cries out. 'We're not clean. Clean? Is our dark skin like dirt to him? Are our faces not white enough?'

The manager appears at the door, likely drawn by Princess's voice and the silence from everyone else. He says nothing. He watches her. Watches us. Waiting to see what's about to happen, I suppose.

People nudge each other. Nod towards him. Princess sees him too. She turns. Raises her hands. Begins to clap. Slowly. Deliberately. Pausing between each clap to give a message. A mocking message.

I hold my breath. I stare at the manager's face, his little

screwed-up eyes, and wonder if he's going to march in and drag Princess out. She's tall. Powerful. He'd have a real fight on his hands. After a moment, a chair scrapes across the floor as Meri stands. She walks over to Princess. She claps too – matching Princess's rhythm exactly. Princess smiles at her. They clap together. Two men stand now and join Princess and Meri. One person becomes four.

More chairs scrape as others stand up, joining the slow clap, hesitantly at first, but gradually getting more confident. Louder. Four people swells to half the canteen. Standing in unison at their tables, in the queue, in the centre of the floor. All clapping. All mocking. It's powerful and it fills my heart.

I stand too to support Princess. To support what's happening here. Mother stands next to me and we clap together. I look across the table as Fiza gets to her feet, smiling. She glares at her parents until eventually even Mrs Farooq stands. Mr Farooq doesn't. He sits silently, eating his chips. The rest of us clap. This is important. This is the first time we have all joined together. All clapping.

The manager's face is red. He no longer watches us. The stools have swopped. Now, *we* watch *him*. Now, we are stronger. Swiftly, he turns and leaves. The slow clapping breaks apart and becomes normal clapping. People laugh and shout support and applaud Princess, who doesn't look any happier. She's still upset. We start talking again. Collect our food. Return to eating. There's high energy in the room. Snatches of conversation about a victory. About joining together.

'What happens now?' Fiza asks. Her father frowns at her and Fiza immediately drops her eyes. Goes quiet.

Princess goes around to the tables, talking to people. She comes to us.

'We need to push our strength today. Show we are unified.'

'I am not jeopardising our application for a traditional meal,' Mr Farooq says

Princess stares at him. I stare at him. Even Fiza stares at him.

'This is not only about a *traditional* meal,' Princess says. Her eyes burn into Mr Farooq. He must feel the heat of her gaze. 'This is about *freedom* to live how we choose. Don't you see? We have no *choice*, no freedom, no *opportunity* as long as we stay in Direct Provision. Some of us are here *years* – wasting our lives away while normal life continues beyond these walls.'

Mr Farooq looks directly at Princess. 'You've already been given a warning. Next, you'll be sent back to your own country. That's not about to happen my family.'

Princess pulls herself up straight as though she has been slapped in the face. 'Standing up for your rights does *not* get you sent home. We have a right to freedom! To be free of degrading and inhuman treatment. To be free of discrimination! These rights are *denied* within these walls. I can't put up with it. We can't put up with it. *Together*, we're all stronger.'

Mr Farooq speaks slowly and quietly, but his words are clear. 'Then you should not stay within these walls,' he says. 'Do as the manager has said. Leave.'

Princess's eyes shine with tears. She screws up her face as though she's trying to hold in her fury and upset.

'There's nothing I want more than to leave,' she says through clenched teeth. 'But right now, there's nowhere I can go.'

She turns and sweeps out of the canteen without collecting her food.

'He made her cry,' Mother whispers to me.

I remember Princess saying how she was rebelling against the rules even in this country. How she hasn't yet found where she fits in. I push my chair back and hurry after her. Glimpse a flash of orange and red as she rounds the landing. I leap up the stairs, catching up with her on the first floor.

'Princess!'

'We've no *freedom* in this place!' she bursts out. Her tears flow freely now. Her voice cracks. 'Why must they clip our wings so we can *never* take flight – and then *pretend* they care for us? They don't care for us! This manager: he only cares for his money. This government: they only care for power. In their greed, they feed us cheap plastic food. Herd us together in these places … these barns … like animals. They control *everything* about our lives like we are *experiments* for them to study.'

She paces the landing, her body agitated, fretting. Her hands wave wildly, sweeping the air. 'And then that man – that awful man who stops his own child speaking because she is a *girl* – thinks it is about traditional *food*?'

'Mr Farooq?'

'He doesn't know the meaning of freedom. His daughters, his wife – they have no freedom even in their own family. Can't speak their opinions. Can't make choices. Women are not *human* in his eyes, Azari!'

I daren't tell Princess that Mr Farooq sleeps in the single bed, while Mrs Farooq sleeps on the floor and the three girls are in the big bed.

'My father is like Mr Farooq,' I say. 'I am only now learning what it means to be free.'

Princess stops her agitation. She stands in front of me. Places her hands on my shoulders and looks into my eyes. 'You haven't even begun to experience true freedom, little Azari-Nike, but you're hungry for it. And for the life you will enjoy because of it. *That's* why it's so important for you to watch out for Fiza too. She might find her own way, but she needs you to lead her.' She drops her hands, and spins on her heel. 'But not within Direct Provision!'

.   .   .

After breakfast on Saturday, I change into running leggings and shorts.

'Azari?' Mother says.

'I'm going running,' I tell her. 'With a friend.'

Mother is working hard to tolerate my running, but sometimes she gets anxious, no matter how much she tries.

'From the Centre?' she asks.

'A student I met in the town library.' I keep my head down. Lace my trainers. I don't look at her.

'An Irish girl?'

I throw a scrunchie in my hair as I look at her conflicting expressions. She's trying to be supportive but isn't happy.

'I won't be long,' I tell her as I kiss her on the cheek. 'Back before lunch.'

'Enjoy yourself,' she says eventually. 'Be safe.'

Robert and I arranged to meet at the new roundabout on the main road. I didn't want to meet him outside the Centre gates – too close for comfort – so I chose somewhere about twenty minutes away.

'You want to meet at a *roundabout*?' he said when I told him. 'Are you sure? I mean I can meet you in a café or the shopping centre.'

'I'm ok with the roundabout. Is it close to you?' I don't know where he lives.

'Yeah, it's grand. Roundabout it is so. I'll be there.'

I'm nervous and excited. I jog down the driveway, loosening up. It's a bright morning and my skin feels the warmth of the sun in a way I've not felt in Ireland. Summer is coming.

Sharnaz starts muttering warnings to me. *I'm not sure this is safe, Azari. Who knows where you are? Who knows you're alone with a boy?*

'Hopefully nobody!' I tell her. 'Don't start, Sharnaz. I've my phone with me. We're out in the open on a sunny morning. Nothing's going to happen.'

How do you know?

'Princess says I have a strong spirit. I'm independent. It's my life. I have rights.'

Sharnaz sniggers. *Listen to you! Rights and independence and strong spirit! Much good they will do you.*

I need to silence my sister before she puts me off. I focus on my warm-up, stretch out my legs. Run hard. I get there with time to spare. Even though I'm early, Robert's there ahead of me, bleached head on him. Running tights, shorts, bright orange running shoes. He looks taller than in the library. Strong legs that tell of running and winning. I already know he's a good runner. I avert my eyes from his tight clothes. Look elsewhere. Mother would have a fit if she knew what I was up to. I smile a little at the thought.

'I've an easy loop worked out for us,' he says, setting his smart watch. 'Till we get to know each other's stride. I've built in a few escape routes if either of us decides to pull out.'

'I won't be pulling out,' I tell him.

He looks at me. 'And there's a couple of low slow hills to push us.'

'What pace?'

'Take it handy to begin with. We won't push ourselves too hard. Good to go?'

'Good to go.'

We head off, curving down the long gentle slope in the direction of town. It feels strange and new to have a running partner. I haven't run with anyone since Ruba, Iman and I ran through the fields and sunny streets around our village. Robert is tall. He stretches his legs out easily, pulling slightly ahead of me. Maybe I should push faster – catch up with him to show I can stay the pace. I increase my speed. He adjusts too. Slows a little. After the first kilometre or so, we match strides and settle into a comfortable pace. Should we talk? Run in silence? In the end, I decide just to enjoy the run for what it is. I relax. Relish the freedom running always brings. We're on the main road, heading towards town. Plenty of people passing in cars, on bicycles. I feel safe. There's something nice about running next to him.

'Look at me now, Sharnaz. Big surprise?' I think. Then I pull myself up and stop my talk to her. I don't want to start her chattering in my head, distracting me. I want to enjoy this time. I focus on my stride.

'Don't make stupid decisions about running with Robert, Azari-Nike,' Princess told me when I asked her about it a few nights ago. 'Stay out in the open. Don't go off somewhere different. Go for your run and come straight back to the Centre afterwards.'

'You think it's OK to go?'

'There's nothing threatening about it. Go! Enjoy your freedom! Enjoy your runs!'

'What will I tell my mother?' I ask.

Princess looked at me. 'Only you can decide that, my friend. It's not for me to tell you what you should say to your own mother.'

As I run back to the Centre from the roundabout later that day, I can't stop smiling inside and out. It was great to be back running properly. I loved it as much as my running club back home. It was fast. Hard. Challenging. I enjoyed Robert's company and easy chat. Now, on the homeward stretch, my muscles are burning.

'How was your run?' Mother says when I get back.

'Great! Having a friend made it better. Like being back in the running club.'

• • •

Robert and I start a routine, meeting for a run on Saturdays. I decide where we'll meet up; he plans the route, timing us on his smart watch. Sometimes the runs are hard and fast and short: sprints interspersed with slower stretches. Mostly they're long and slow. He throws in a few hills to challenge us. Changes the scenery to keep it interesting. Sometimes we run along the busy main road, sometimes quiet country lanes. We do a couple of runs along the river, following an old railway track busy with cyclists and walkers and other runners.

The weather throws all manner of seasons at us, even though the Irish people call it summer, which Mother and I think is funny. Rain, sun, hail, cloud, cold. I arrive back to the Centre sometimes wet, sometimes blue with cold, sometimes sweating.

After several weeks, I dare to give Robert my phone number, then lie awake all that night, worried he'll stalk me.

He doesn't stalk me. If we don't catch each other in the town library during the week, he messages me Friday evenings to check I'm OK to run. I'm almost always OK to run. Saturdays can't come around quick enough.

The only time I don't run with him is when I'm unclean. Even though the information leaflets say it's good to exercise, it still doesn't seem right. At home, Mother sent me to scour the rubbish dump. Told me not to cook or bathe. Those feelings of being unclean haven't changed. I feel uncomfortable about running with a boy, but it feels doubly wrong to spend time alone with Robert when I'm impure. What happens if I have an accident and he finds out? I'd never be able to talk to him again! Though now I'm getting free supplies from the library and the supermarket, I feel less anxious about accidents.

When we run, Robert pushes us hard. My old strength returns. My muscles regain definition and power. Running holds the same magic as it did in the dusty streets around my little school and village. It brings alive something inside me: something bright that was quenched a long time ago. Like a huge bubble, filling me with happiness I hardly remember. Those couple of hours make all other hours in the Centre and school easier to get through. I'm sleeping through the night: I haven't heard Meri snacking on her crackers or Mother snoring for weeks. Best of all, my golden dreams of running and competing have returned.

'I'm doing it for you, Sharnaz.' I tell her of our latest routes and how good it feels to be back running.

Never mind me! You need to tell Mother, Azari, Sharnaz says. *The longer it goes on, the harder it becomes.*

'I don't know how to break it to her,' I say.

But it turns out I don't need to: someone else tells her first.

Chapter 11

When I get back from my Saturday run, Mother gives me a letter with the official stamp of the IPO on it.

My stomach drops. 'Where did you get this?'

'The manager.'

'There's no post on Saturday. He's had this since *yesterday*!'

We've been waiting months for our letter from the IPO. Waiting for a response to our questionnaire and Sheila's letter. I've tried to put the endless waiting out of my head. Tried to live by Sharnaz's advice: *think only of today, Azari. Not last year. Or next week. Or next month. Only today. Get through today.* I've checked the post every day when I got back to the Centre from school. Asked the manager whenever I've seen him if there have been any phone calls, any letters. The answer is always no. No. No. And now, when the letter finally does arrive, he holds it overnight and doesn't even tell us about it.

'Is it the one we're waiting for?' Mother asks.

'That's it.' The next step.

I tear it open. Scan the information. 'Our interview's in six weeks. We've to travel to the city. We've to let the IPO know we're going to attend.' I look up at Mother. I'm nervous. 'This is a very important part of our asylum application. It's where they decide our future.'

She looks at me, her face creased with worry. She gets upset whenever there's official business to do with our application. This is such a big step, it has a bigger impact. She doesn't want to speak about it. Doesn't want to know any more. She retreats to her bed for three days, which she hasn't done for a long time. She doesn't even want to come down for dinner to complain about the food with Mrs Farooq. I worry about her, on top of worrying about preparing for the interview. My sleep is broken and restless again.

Sheila already told us she can't help with this part. Mother won't travel a long distance for legal aid. I must find someone closer who can help us. I ask some women in the Centre if they know where I can find information about someone local.

'Ask in the library,' they say. 'They have numbers.'

Next day in the town library, I look around to make sure no-one from school is here: I don't want this to become school gossip. When I see it's quiet, I go up to the librarian.

'I'm looking for legal aid.' I keep my voice down.

'What kind?' she asks. 'Is it for yourself?'

'International protection,' I say. My face burns. 'To prepare for the interview.'

The librarian smiles. 'I'll see what I have.'

She finds a leaflet with names and numbers on it.

'Are any of these in town?' I ask her.

'I don't think so.' She scans the leaflet. 'But some are close by. Just a short bus ride away. Will I mark them for you?'

By the time I leave to catch the school bus, I have the names of three solicitors working in nearby towns: two women, one man. I start by calling the women. The first solicitor isn't seeing new people. The woman who answers the phone asks me to call back in six months. I leave a message on the second solicitor's answering machine, with my mobile number. I miss her return call when I'm in school, but ring her from the payphone when I get back to the Centre.

'You sound young,' she says. 'Have you an adult with you in Ireland?'

'My mother,' I tell her. 'But she doesn't speak English.'

The solicitor makes an appointment to meet me in a few days' time.

'Your mother must come, even if she has little English,' she says. 'And bring all documents and letters you have.'

'I'm not going to any more of these appointments,' Mother says when I tell her.

'It's not far this time,' I say. 'The next town. We can get a bus after lunch and be back for dinner. Please, Mother. I'm not allowed on my own and we need help with this part.'

She finally agrees, though not without more complaining and another day in the bed. The following Wednesday, we get a bus to meet Liz, our new legal aid solicitor.

'Are you missing school today?' she asks right away.

'Half day on Wednesday,' I say.

'Good. Your schooling is too important. No skipping, you hear?'

Liz is older than Sheila and a lot bossier. She doesn't ask our opinion so much. She decides exactly what's going to happen and when. She immediately organises an interpreter on the phone. A woman.

'I expect you and your mother to attend all appointments,' Liz says. 'Strict time limits apply at all stages of the asylum process and if you fail to attend any appointments, legal aid won't be able to provide you with a service. Is that clear?'

'Yes, Miss,' I say. I feel like I'm speaking to a teacher.

Liz is a bit scary, but she knows exactly how these interviews go. She reads the letter from the IPO.

'I see your mother refused to speak to the IPO the last time,' she says, looking over her glasses at me. 'Is this likely to happen again?'

I look at Mother, then nod my head.

Liz frowns. 'This might be a problem. It would be very unusual for you to be interviewed as a minor. All I can do is request it.'

She makes notes on the pad in front of her.

'All our appointments will be through an interpreter, even though your English is reasonably good. We'll use the same one all the time, and practise so you're used to telling your story. Of course, the IPO will use their own interpreter. And we'll request a female case-worker. You'd probably be more comfortable with a woman, instead of a man.' She looks at me. 'Am I right?'

I nod. If it's going to be as difficult as everyone says, having a female case-worker might make things a little better, especially as we are two women alone. What male official would believe the story of unaccompanied women against another man?

Liz reads through the documents I brought. Takes a photocopy of everything before handing them back.

'Your personal interview is your chance to tell the IPO why you had to leave home and why it's unsafe for you to return. I'll be with you during it, but I can't answer the questions. It's your story and you need to tell it. The case-worker will write down everything and then read it back to you, so you can check it's exactly what you want to say. You can add more information or details if you like. Any questions?'

'Is it like the first interview?'

'More detailed. A lot more information is required. I'll work with you to agree your story and your mother's story. It won't be easy, Azari. You'll have to talk about what happened to you. Details of upsetting things. And we'll have to try and get your mother's account recorded too. It's a bit thin at the moment.'

'What happens then?'

'The IPO will make their first-instance decision. That takes a long time to come through. Months. Even years sometimes. During that time, they might ask questions or look for clarification.'

'What do we do?'

Liz sighs. 'That's the hardest part. You'll be in Direct Provision. Trying to get on with your life, even with this shadow over everything you do, every decision you make. It's not good, but there's no other way.'

Liz arranges to meet us again in two weeks.

'I'll have read everything by then,' she says. 'We'll make a few appointments to talk until I'm satisfied we're fully prepared.'

We get back to the Centre for dinner and Mother is hungry for the first time in days.

. . .

It's Saturday. Summer. Lashing rain. Robert and I cut short our run when a downpour comes at us sideways, stinging our faces and blinding us with its ferocity.

After lunch, sheets of water wash in rivers across the concrete yard. It's hard to see where the ground ends and the clouds start. Mother and I eye the bulging bag of laundry in the corner of our room.

'I'm not queuing outside in that,' I say.

'We'll do it by hand in the bathroom,' she says. 'Nobody will know.'

To stop people washing clothes, there are no plugs in the wash-hand basins. I block the plugholes with wadded plastic bags, and while Mother washes, I rinse the clothes in clean water. We'll hang them to drip-dry across the window and over the radiator later. We're not supposed to dry clothes in our rooms, but everyone does it. Nobody wants to queue in the yard in bad weather.

At home, we washed clothes on the washing stones by the river: groups of women chattering and scrubbing until our shoulders ached and our hands were raw. We hung our washing on the mulberry bushes in our yard and gathered it in that evening, bone dry and smelling of sunshine, but that can't happen here.

'How are you getting on with your new running friend?' Mother asks.

I'm careful in my reply. 'Fine. I like having someone to run with. It makes it easier.'

'You go for long runs together,' she says. 'You sure you're safe?'

'We only run along busy routes where there are lots of people,' I tell her. 'We're safe. And I have my phone with me.'

'You've got used to everything being so different here,' Mother says. 'How will you manage without this freedom when we go home? Those things will stop then. No phone. No running.'

'*When*?' I glance at her. 'We might never go back, Mother.'

She shakes her head, as though she knows differently. Her words cast a shadow over my heart. Our future is so uncertain. Even after our IPO interview, we'll be waiting months, years, according to Liz. Our whole lives will be taken up with waiting.

'This is where we live now, Mother. In Ireland. Home is far away.'

'This isn't living,' Mother says. 'It isn't normal life. All these months of waiting and doing nothing and even after all that, they might still send us home. What will you say to your father then?'

I can't imagine we might end up going back home. My life there seems so long ago. It's coming up on a year since we left. So much has happened. In my head and my heart, our previous life is over. I hope we stay in Ireland. I hope I can run without being told it's not for women. But what if Mother is right? What if we get deported after all this time? Now she's put her thoughts out into the universe, anything could happen.

I'm almost the same age Sharnaz was when she died. I'm a different person than the girl who fled my village at dawn with my injured sister. I feel so much more than one year older. I'm stronger. Wiser. I have more freedom and choices than ever before. I also have more limits and restrictions than ever before.

'Do you really want to go home, Mother?' I ask. 'Back to what we left behind?'

She drops the shirt she's scrubbing into the soapy water. Shakes her head and stares as though reading the soap bubbles. 'It's a question I ask myself a hundred times a day, Azari, when I'm alone in this cold, dark place and you're nowhere near. The answer is carved into the darkest corner of my heart: I want to be home more than life itself. I want to look into the eyes of my beautiful sons and see their forgiveness. I want to sleep beside my husband, in spite of his faults and weaknesses. I want to breathe the air of our village and heal my broken heart. Only then can I die in peace.'

Her words cut through me like a knife and I don't know what to say. Part of me wants nothing to do with the village and my life there, but another part of me aches for my home, my brothers. My sister more than anybody. Everything that made me who I am. I don't want to stay in this Centre where I'm missing out on normal life, but I'm also clear I don't want to go home.

'My life as I knew it is over,' Mother says. 'I can't go back to something torn to shreds. None of what we had remains. My dreams will never come true. My heart will never heal.' She faces me, eyes full of sadness. 'I watch you growing farther and farther from me every day, Azari. You're young. You're learning. Life is a new adventure for you, but the distance between us frightens me. You're not the girl who left with me. What will I have when that girl is gone for ever? How will I manage alone in this strange country?'

'I'm not going anywhere, Mother. We came to Ireland together. We'll stay together. I'll always be here with you.'

Mother whispers. 'I can't manage without you. You have life outside this prison. I have nothing. I hardly know you any more. Our lives are no longer one, as they were at home.'

Guilt twists my stomach. She's right. For weeks, I've not been open and honest with her. I've kept Robert a secret. It doesn't feel right, but I'm afraid she'll stop my running. It's not only me: Fiza doesn't tell her parents her secrets either, in case they stop her doing normal things everyone in Ireland does. Living in two worlds as different as lemons and mangoes is harder than ever.

'I don't mean to, Mother.' I take a breath. 'I'm afraid.'

'I won't beat you, Azari, or send you to sleep outside.' She wipes wet hands on her dress. 'What are you afraid of?'

What am I afraid of? Her reaction when she hears I'm running with a boy. A white Irish boy. Messaging him on my phone. Meeting him in the library after school.

'Disappointing you.'

'You will never disappoint me,' she says.

'I'm not the same as I was. You said it yourself. It's hard to be true to our traditional customs in Ireland. Everything is different here. I can't stay the same. I stand out too much.'

'I can't bear being alone with nobody to talk to,' she says. 'Not knowing your life makes it so much harder. I might not like what I hear, but I'd prefer to know. I've always known what you're up to, but no more.'

My eyes prick with tears. How I've hurt my mother is unforgivable. My own flesh and blood. The one person who has given up everything – *everything* – for me. I'm being selfish.

'I won't leave you alone at weekends,' I blurt out. 'I'll stop running so I can be with you.'

Her short laugh startles me. 'Give up running? Don't be ridiculous, Azari! Sharnaz *wanted* this for you. She gave her life for your freedom. I don't want you to stop running – it's taken me until now to give you my blessing. I'm not Mrs Farooq.' She takes a deep breath. 'I only want that you *talk* to me.'

I smile at her. I'd give up my running in a heartbeat to make her happier but I'm so relieved I don't have to.

We carry our damp washing back to the room. Meri is watching videos in a foreign language on her phone. She ignores us as we hang damp clothes. The windows are already dripping with condensation which is about to get a whole lot worse.

Guilt weighs heavy on my chest. I take Mother's hand and draw her to the bed. We sit beside each other. She looks at me, questioning.

'The friend I run with on Saturdays is an Irish teenager I met in the library,' I say carefully.

Mother nods.

'It's not a girl.' I send a silent prayer up to Sharnaz. 'I run with a boy.'

'I know.'

My heart skips a beat. 'You *know*?'

'You think I hear nothing. Talk to nobody.' She nods. 'I've known for weeks. I've been waiting for you to tell me.'

How did mother find out? Names run through my head. 'Did Mr Farooq tell you? Mrs Farooq?'

Mother shakes her head no.

'Not Princess? Or Fiza?'

'Not them.'

I'm running out of names. I look back at our room-mate, chuckling away at her videos.

'Meri?' I whisper.

'Not Meri.'

'Tell me then.'

'The manager.'

'The *Centre* manager?' That makes no sense. Why would he tell Mother my business? How does he even *know* my business?

'The day the letter arrived from the IPO, he came to the room.' I remember the day clearly: Mother showing me the letter. Me being annoyed he gave it to us a day late. 'He said you were out running with your boy and to give it to you when you got back.'

My face burns with shame and embarrassment. 'He's not my *boy*. He's a friend, Mother. Nothing more. He's a boy who runs with me.' I'm mortified. 'You believe me, don't you?'

'You're a good girl, Azari.' She takes my hands. 'I'm not happy about your spending time alone with a boy. A white Irish boy at that. Your Father would lose his reason if he knew. It's not how you were brought up. Can you imagine the village council if this was known at home?'

I drop my eyes. I can't look her in the face. Mother goes on.

'You should never have kept this from me, Azari. Secrets are something shameful. Something wrong. Something that can't be shared. You kept this secret because you knew I wouldn't approve.'

'I felt ashamed,' I say. 'Sharnaz said I should tell you, but I didn't know how. The weeks went on and it got harder and harder.'

'Sharnaz?' Mother looks at me.

'I talk to her. In my head. She was cross because I didn't tell you.'

'She was such a good daughter. So obedient and thoughtful.' She looks at me. 'But you have spirit and adventure in you. That makes you Azari.' She takes my hands. 'I am learning to accept your running because we are in Ireland. Everything is different here. In time, I might learn to accept you have Irish friends outside the Centre – friends who are not only girls. It might be normal in Ireland, but it will take me time to come around. I'm not ready to give you my blessing to run with this boy but promise me you will keep your honour in his company.'

I'm shocked Mother even thinks she has to say this. 'Of course! I've done *nothing* to bring shame on myself or you. I've only ever run with him in public.'

'Never keep secrets from me, Azari. It's too hard on me. You are my world and I always wish love and blessings on you.'

I hold her tightly, my love for her spilling out of my heart and filling my eyes. 'I'm relieved you know at last. I'm sorry for not telling you.'

'You know I don't agree with it, but I've said my piece. And if we ever go back home, I won't be telling anyone.'

'Not even Aunt Hania?' I wink at Mother.

'Especially Aunt Hania. Now,' she says. 'Let's finish hanging these clothes.'

We shake out the remainder of our washing.

'Where did the manager even see me?' I ask.

'You crossed the road in front of his car near a road circle.'

'The roundabout,' I say. 'That's where we start our runs sometimes.'

Sometimes, in strange ways, this Centre is not so unlike my village at home.

'And you understood all this news about me when he told you? Your English is getting better, Mother.'

'I make sure to understand important news.'

. . .

Together, Fiza and I read the whole book for the book club. She helps me with the hard words and I understand more and more as we go on. We both really get into the story. It's nothing like work-at-home. It's exciting! My heart nearly bursts near the end when the smallest boy falls out of their boat and we think he's drowned in the sea. He reminds me of my little brothers at home. The book finishes with the whole family kneeling on a stony beach.

'How do we find out what happens next?' I ask Fiza.

She shrugs. 'Maybe ask the book club?'

I'm so relieved Mother and I didn't have to escape in a small boat. And I'm very proud I've read a whole book in English. I even want to read another one.

We have a little party for the last book-club meeting of the school year. We're not usually allowed food and drink in the school library, but the librarian makes an exception on this occasion and provides us with plastic cups and orange juice. Emer brings a whole apple pie, and other girls bring in chocolate muffins, popcorn and crisps. It's fun. We talk over all the books the book club read throughout the year – though of course I joined so late I only got to read the last one – and what we want to read next year. I tell them I didn't like the ending of the book I read because I want to know what happens to the family next.

'Wanting to know more of the story is always the sign of a good book,' says the librarian. 'Can you recommend any books about your country for us to read, Azari?'

'I can find out,' I say. 'And let you know.'

In my head, I'm thinking Fiza will probably have suggestions for me.

Chapter 12

After school breaks up for the summer, Robert and I run once, sometimes twice, a week. Since he's no longer a secret, my running is better than ever. Lighter. Faster. Easier. I didn't realise how much it was weighing me down.

Even Robert notices, though he doesn't know why. 'Hey, Az, you're in good form.'

'Amn't I always?' I say. We're comfortable with each other now.

'Never! You're usually a narky cow,' he says with a grin. 'But you're definitely different. Kinda springier.'

Springier. I say the word to myself. It's a good word. Describes how I feel.

While I might be springier, Princess is definitely not. Since the manager banned any hope of Soul Food, she has been quiet and withdrawn. She's no longer such a strong presence. There have been no meetings. Princess is not like Mother – she doesn't take to the bed – but she has become a little distant. Not as sparkling and vivid as she was, even though her coloured dresses are as bright as ever. I've tried to cheer her up and she tells me she's doing OK, but I see a difference in her.

Things haven't changed in the Centre, but Mother and I are close and strong, which makes everything better. Running and focussing on our personal interview helps fill the long boring days when there's no bus into town, no book club, no chat after school in the library. I hang around all day with nothing to do, sometimes with Fiza but more often not. Her mother doesn't like her spending too much time with me, in case I'm a bad influence, so she keeps her precious daughter busy with chores and caring for her little sisters. This means I'm left with my own thoughts a little too much. They go around my head, tormenting me. I fret about our interview. Worry I'll say the wrong thing. Or not say enough. Everything – our whole future – rests on how it goes.

Mother and I have met Liz four times now. We've never missed an appointment, though Liz sees nothing of the endless arguments I have with my mother to get her to come each time. I've got used to Liz's bossiness and see how good she is. She asks me questions over and over. Guides me in my answers. Tells me when I don't go into enough detail or when something isn't clear. My story is tight and strong. We've captured everything from Mother's view as well and Liz helps me to weave Mother's version into my own story.

'Tell the truth,' she says. 'Always tell the truth and you'll never trip yourself up. Your story is powerful enough to stand on its own without adding extra things that never happened.'

As I recall what happened to us and tell it over and over to Liz, memories crowd into my thoughts, filling my head with their loud mutterings and cries. At night, my dreams are soaked with the colours and sounds of our last days in the village, filling my heart with longing for my sister and my golden life before I became a woman. In darker nights, I smell the jasmine blossoms at the sacred pool. Feel the soft ash of our burned field under my feet. The touch of Sharnaz's cold hand on the evening of her henna party. Frequently, sleep is ripped from me and my eyes fly open. Heart pounding, sweating, I lie staring at the ceiling, wishing for nothing more than to see Sharnaz's face again. To hear her soft voice.

As I count down the days to the anniversary of what should have been the eve of her wedding, the last day I saw my beautiful sister alive and well, the pain of her loss and her wasted dreams crushes me. One year on, I'm overwhelmed with grief. Shocked by the physical pain of sadness, I lie in bed in the Centre, too heartbroken to face the long summer days. I even cancel a couple of runs with Robert.

Mother strokes my hair as I sob into my pillow.

'I'll never see her again. Never hear her again.'

'Hush now,' she says. 'Sharnaz will always be in our hearts. She won't ever leave you.'

When I lie in the darkness of night, unable to sleep and utterly alone, Sharnaz visits me, whispering words of comfort and cradling me in her heart.

I'll never leave you, little Azari. I'm still here. I'm watching over you.

And I truly believe she is.

· · ·

The day of our personal interview comes towards the end of the summer. Almost a year since we arrived in Ireland. The day is exhausting and upsetting and endless. After an early start, a two-hour walk and two buses, we finally arrive at the same IPO we visited to register for international protection a year previously. Liz is there ahead of us, with armfuls of documents. She introduces us to our female case-worker, stony-faced and dry, pen and paper in front of her.

'We got your letter asking us to interview a child instead of an adult,' the case-worker says to Liz. 'It's not something the IPO can accommodate.'

'The IPO accommodated it at the preliminary interview,' says Liz.

The case-worker raises her eyebrows as though she doesn't believe Liz. 'The daughter was interviewed instead?'

She leafs through her notes while Liz waits patiently. The case-worker pulls out a page and scans it, reading out words here and there. 'Exceptional circumstances … not normally permitted … agreed with the applicant …' She looks at Liz. 'Well, this is most unusual.'

'As the notes state, "exceptional circumstances,"' Liz says. 'I take it the IPO will accommodate our request on this occasion too?'

The case-worker stiffens in her seat.

'I suppose so,' she says, and then dials up the interpreter.

The preparation with Liz has straightened our story in my head, but I'm not prepared for how it knots my heart and wrenches my soul. Perhaps it's because I've told it so often. Or because the case-worker seems so cold. Or because Sharnaz is gone from us a year, but when I start to speak, I'm not only *telling* the story: I'm back in the hot village streets.

I watch the baying crowd yell and howl as they drag Sharnaz through the dust and fling her in our yard. Deeba and her dark-skinned sisters scream insults and hurl clods of earth. Old women spit and curse every woman in our family.

I sit in our yard, leaning against the rough boards of the outhouse. Sharnaz sleeps in my lap, my arms holding the weight of her. The sky is black but for a ribbon of twinkling light weaving across the heavens. Mosquitoes whine in my ear. Tiny creatures rustle in the night. I rest my head back. Close my eyes until Mother appears beside me, whispering urgently.

I stand waist-deep in the sacred pool, dark water cool and soothing for my sister, lifting her weight and easing her pain. Colour seeps into the dawn, bringing danger and my sister's final breath closer. When she has left this world, her face is peaceful at last, her eyes closed. I let her go and she sinks beneath the surface to sleep in the soft mud below, under the watch of the stone goddess.

I crouch on the bus with Mother, lurching towards town. Numb, uncertain, heartbroken. We've no plan. No safe place to go. Komal meets us. Then Yalina. There's hope. And terror.

And fear. We take our chances because we have to: we have no choice.

After many days of darkness and fear, white men find us among the crates and cargo, shivering and frightened and cold. So cold. We're in Ireland. Far from home. Yalina said to ask for international protection. International protection …

'Azari?' The voice startles me.

I blink. Look around in surprise at the grey office I sit in. I'm no longer in our little village. I'm in Ireland. In the IPO for my interview. I don't know how long I've been talking or what time it is.

'Are you OK?' Liz leans forward in her chair, her gaze locked on me. 'Would you like a glass of water?'

'I'm OK.'

Mother has her headscarf across her face, eyes shining with tears. The case-worker holds her pen. She stares at me. She doesn't look so dry any more. Finally, she clears her throat.

'Is that everything?' she says.

I glance at Liz, who nods.

'That's everything,' I say.

'I'm now going to read back what you told us, so you can check it's accurate,' the case-worker says. 'You can make any corrections or give more detail, if you like.'

Liz interrupts the case-worker. 'My client is in no fit state to continue with this interview. I'm requesting we break at this point. Perhaps the written account could be sent to my office? I'll review it with Azari and return a signed copy to you.'

The case-worker looks at Liz. 'This is not a regular request.'

'This is not a regular situation,' Liz says.

'The IPO has already made significant accommodation for your client,' the case-worker says. 'In breach of usual procedures.'

'You can see Azari is not fit to continue. She needs rest and time to recover.' Liz's voice has an edge to it. She stands up. 'I am terminating this interview for medical reasons.'

The case-worker stares at Liz. She looks at me.

'I need my manager to approve this request,' she says.

'It's not a request,' Liz says as the case-worker hurries from the room.

Things happen swiftly after that. The case-worker's manager approves sending the written account to Liz's office. The interview ends at last.

'You'll hear from us in due course,' says the case-worker as we leave the IPO.

It's bright and sunny when we get outside but everything is off-kilter for me. I'm not fully back in this world yet. I shiver. Liz is concerned; she keeps looking at me closely. When she speaks, her voice is distant, echoing strangely in my head.

'We need to get you back to the Centre. That took a lot out of you.'

Mother points in the direction of the bus-stop. Pulls my arm.

'I can't let Azari get two buses back to town and then walk all the way from there,' Liz says. 'She's not well. I've my car parked around the corner and am driving back to the office anyway. I'll give you both a lift.'

As soon as I'm in the car, I fall asleep. I don't wake up until Mother shakes me when we arrive at the Centre. I've no memory of getting out of the car or saying goodbye to Liz. When I wake again properly, it's dark outside. I don't know where the day has gone.

'I was getting worried about you,' Mother says.

I sit up. 'I'm starving.'

'You missed dinner,' Mother says. 'But I brought you food.'

My head is clear, and I feel better than I have in days. I wolf down the jam sandwich and apple Mother sneaked up to the room.

.   .   .

It's a relief to go back to school in September, if only to have something to fill the empty days. A new girl from Eritrea has arrived in the Centre and she joins us in Black School, bringing our number to nine. I move up to second year with the same class of girls, who are as excitable and mad as ever. Emer is now in Transition Year and comes flying up to me in the corridor in the first week to say hello and to tell me the date of our first book-club meeting.

I also see the Irish girls who were nasty to me before the summer. They snigger and point at me, hissing insults under their breath, but I stick with girls from my class and ignore them. I also take comfort in knowing I'm not the only one being picked on: there's talk in the Centre most evenings about locals making racist comments to asylum seekers. Telling people they're not welcome.

'I saw a poster in the library about a meeting to close the Centre,' I tell Princess one evening.

She looks shocked. 'Who organised it?'

'Dunno, but they want us moved out of town. Will I take a picture on my phone to show you?'

But when I go back to the library the next day, the poster has been taken down. I don't see it again, but stories about racist comments and hostile towns-people keep coming. Some shops have notices in the windows banning people from the Centre.

'That's not allowed,' Fiza says. 'That's discrimination. It's against the law.'

Most of the time, I ignore it all and get on with other stuff. Robert and I keep running on Saturdays, building our distance and our speed. We're even talking about taking part in a half-marathon, which I'm excited about. Fiza and I start reading a brilliant new book for the book club about a boy in India who's snatched from his family to fight in a war. I meet Liz to review the typed-up account from my personal interviews. Mother doesn't even have to come this time. Liz is still bossy, but now I know her better, I see she's kind and concerned about me.

'I couldn't let you get a bus that day,' she says. 'You looked like death warmed up.'

I thank her for ending the interview early and for giving us a lift back to the Centre.

'What happens now?' I ask.

'We wait. And wait. And wait. Remember what I said before, Azari: it takes many months, sometimes years. I'll contact the IPO every couple of months, just to keep the pressure on. If I have any news, I'll let you know.'

•   •   •

The evenings close in earlier and days are cooler. Hallowe'en is coming. Here in Ireland, Hallowe'en is a time of fireworks and bonfires, of bangers and firecrackers and loud noises. Of great excitement and terrible frights and dangerous things. We don't have Hallowe'en at home. We have fireworks and bonfires, but only as part of celebrations: festivals and weddings. There's no single night when the dead wander among the living, bringing malevolence and evil. When ghosts of the dead are free to roam the earth. This terrifies Mother. Her ghosts are restless and agitated, casting her into strange dark moods. She's been saying for days that something terrible is about to happen.

'The distance between us is shrinking,' she frets. 'They're clamouring to walk among us.'

'Don't let them,' I say. 'I don't want your ghosts walking among us.'

'Then we'll pray to keep us safe,' she says. 'And we'll fast too.'

Hallowe'en for us will be a night of prayer and fasting and early to bed.

For the last two weeks, the boys in town have been setting off bangers and firecrackers before and after school. They're banned in school, but as soon as any of us sets foot outside the school gates, we're fair game. The streets in the afternoons are a war zone of explosions and shooting sparks, screams and smoke. The boys mainly target town girls, who burst out of school in tight groups, laughing and screaming. I'm not a town girl and I'm mostly on my own, so they ignore me. I put my head down, wrap my arms around my schoolbag and speedwalk away as fast as possible.

Everything changes in the last week before mid-term. The smokers, the messers, the dossers gather in the square where the bus collects the Centre kids. The crowd of Irish kids gets bigger each day. They shout insults about our skin colour and where we should go – stuff I've heard a million times.

'Stay on the Black Bus and don't come back. We don't want yous here.'

'Spongers. Looking for your free handouts – go back to where yous came from.'

'Fugees! You should be locked up and the key thrun away.'

They throw screwed-up chip bags at us. Empty cans. Bangers.

One afternoon, one of the Irish kids lights a Squealer the wrong way; it shoots towards us, skittering along the ground instead of up in the air, shrieking and popping and fizzing. We hop and jump, scattering like starlings. The town gang cracks up laughing.

·　　·　　·

The evening before school breaks up for mid-term, I'm in the TV room with Mother and Fiza. It's dark outside when a small kid playing in the hall comes running in.

'There's a fire in the garden,' she shouts.

Mother goes to the window as Fiza and I rush to the front door along with half a dozen people. Through the trees, down by the gate, something is ablaze. The night is lit up with a bright glow and the air is full of the smell of smoke and something I don't recognise.

'Petrol,' says a man standing next to me. 'That was started deliberately.'

We stare at the blaze. Staff ring the fire brigade. Parents call their children up to their rooms. Make sure they're safe and nowhere near the fire.

Firefighters arrive to extinguish the flames, then come inside and talk to us. It turns out a large bush inside the gates was set alight but there's nobody around. Nothing to say how it happened, except for the smell of petrol lingering in the air. The firefighters ask us what we saw, how it caught fire, but nobody knows. Nobody saw anything. Within an hour, it's all over.

'Was that it, Mother?' I say as we go to bed that night. 'Was that your ghosts' prophecy – the terrible thing?'

But Mother shakes her head. 'No, Azari, that's not it. It's still out there. It has yet to happen.'

·   ·   ·

The next morning, I gaze out the rain-spattered window of the bus at the charred and blackened bush, the ring of scorched grass. Deep wheel ruts from the fire engine cut into the mud.

A shout goes up from the front of the bus. 'Look at that!'

The wall outside the Centre has been spray-painted with big red letters.

- *No spongers here!*
- *Migrants, go home!*

Racist words too. The whole bus falls silent as we roll past. For the first time, I don't feel safe here.

That afternoon, school breaks up for mid-term. Gangs of teens gather outside the chipper with batter burgers and spice bags and cans. The smell of chips and vinegar and trouble in the air. I've a bad feeling. Maybe I'm starting to hear Mother's ghosts.

The bangers start first. It's more than a bit of *craic* to get us jumping. It's something else. Something darker. It's them flinging fireworks at us: them against us. And they're the only ones with the weapons. It's not only ordinary bangers neither. They've Black Cats and Squealers. The big fireworks. Expensive ones, howling and blasting and zipping around our feet, trailing showers of sparks and smoke. The smaller Centre kids bawl and squeal. We're all hopping and dancing. Squealers shoot into the sky right next to us, screaming and exploding above our heads. Dusk fills with orange banger smoke and showers of sparks.

The Centre kids bunch up together, the older ones cursing and swearing. Some of us tell the swearers to shut up or we'll be the troublemakers and it'll be another thing about us. I don't curse or swear and I'm not shouting at them to shut up. I'm huddling down with Fiza and we're both trying to stay small and unnoticeable and safe.

'Don't matter what we do,' says a tall brown boy with a buzz cut. He's shouting at our attackers, spitting at them. Giving as good as he's getting. 'We'll still get into trouble for it anyhow. Might as well fight back.'

Beyond the smoke and sparks, the twilight is split with cat-calls and shrieks. Some of the kids from the Centre are worked up – crying and screaming. Maybe they've already seen real explosions in their home countries. Maybe they don't know the bangs and shooting sparks are just noisy, but mostly harmless.

At last the bus rolls around the corner. The doors open and a panicked group of Centre kids rushes on, shoving and shouting. Tripping and falling over. Seán is driving. Grumpy at the best of times but now, when he sees the rush of us, he completely loses it.

'Back off! Back off!' he shouts. We ignore him and launch down the aisle. He bellows like a bull. 'What are you doing? Wait your turn. Do yous not learn manners in your countries? Yous are savages, the lot of you.'

Raw eggs smash against the windows of the bus followed by half-eaten burgers slathered with red sauce. A well-aimed Black Cat lands in the doorway, the explosion enough to wake the dead if they weren't already getting up for Hallowe'en. Half of us dive behind the seats with the bang, shouting and shaking. Some of us giggle with nerves: we're safely inside now.

Seán is like a madman but not at us any more. He jumps off the bus after the town kids, roaring and shaking his fist. There's a break in the explosions as the crowd eye him up. Bangers start up again but they're no longer aimed at us. They're being thrown randomly. Seán climbs onto the bus, red-faced and sweating. He kicks the burnt scraps of Black Cat off the step. Shuts the doors. We're away back to the Centre.

'It was terrible today,' I tell Mother later. 'Are your ghosts satisfied now?'

She shakes her head. 'The wall between our worlds is thin and fragile. My ghosts are waiting and watching.'

What more could possibly happen? For the first time ever, a tiny part of me thinks perhaps – just this once – Mother is wrong.

But I should've known better.

·   ·   ·

We're off school for a week and it's a relief to all the students in the Centre. By the time we go back, Hallowe'en will be over for another year.

Hallowe'en itself is damp and misty, with a chill in the air. The greyness doesn't lift. Mother is in a strange mood, sinking beneath currents of darkness. Fretting and agitated, she hardly wants to talk except to tell of her hauntings.

'Spirits are stirring up all manner of pain and heartache. Knocking on the door of my heart.'

'Well, at least we can give them a clean room to visit,' I say.

I strip our bed and collect fresh sheets. Sign out the cleaning trolley. Mother is always better when she has something to keep her hands busy, and before long, she joins me. She holds up the bottle of bleach and the cream cleaner.

'Which is for the mirror?'

'Neither.' I point to the trolley. 'Pink bottle.'

'How can all this dirt build up in one tiny room?'

Meri doesn't let us clean her side of the room, even if we don't touch her stuff. She won't clean it herself either. The floor is tacky. Dirty tissues, old water bottles, food wrappers are scattered under her bed, covered in dust. She stores her clothes in black plastic bin-liners, split and overflowing. The shelf behind her bed is empty so I wipe away sticky marks and dust. Meri's still in bed, grumbling and growling. She throws herself around to show her annoyance. When I start the vacuum cleaner, she glares at me, then pulls the covers over her head.

I open the window to freshen the room and Meri sits bolt upright, a wild head of hair on her. She shouts something in her language and points at the window. Gives me one of her stares. 'You mad!'

At the same time, Mother hurries over. 'Close it! Close it!' She slams the window shut.

Meri disappears under the duvet again, muttering darkly. I don't know which of them surprises me most. The door and windows in our home were always open to the yard.

'You like fresh air,' I say to Mother. 'You didn't mind yesterday.'

'Yesterday wasn't Hallowe'en, Azari,' Mother whispers. 'Yesterday something bad was farther away. The dead are calling. Something bad is happening tonight.'

That evening, we sit with the Farooqs in the canteen even though Mother and I are fasting. Mother and Mrs Farooq complain about the Centre food – their favourite conversation.

'What's this?' Mrs Farooq lifts orange food from the plastic container.

'Orange sauce beans and square fried potatoes,' Mother says.

'Baked beans and waffles,' I say. 'And fish-fingers. It's Friday.'

The menu is the same every week.

'Fish in orange blocks?' Mrs Farooq says. 'Unnatural.'

'How can beans be in orange sauce?' Mother asks.

'Too greasy by far,' says Mrs Farooq. 'The cook uses too much oil. Not smoking hot. If he used a little oil and smoked it, we would have better fingers of fish.'

'Coriander and curry leaves, a little turmeric and cumin to bring out the flavour,' says Mother.

I'm relieved when Princess waves from the other side of the canteen and I can leave our table. Today, she's wearing a headscarf of sunshine yellow with bright green leaves splashed all over it and a dress of the same yellow fabric, like a sunflower. She sits tall, long painted nails drawing her words in the air, bangles jangling on her wrists.

'Have you been running today, Azari?' she asks. 'You need to get out of this place and clear your head. Every. Single. Day.'

'Not today,' I say.

'Fields and woods and roads for miles.' She sweeps her hands towards the window. 'All for running, right?'

I smile. 'Tomorrow.'

I don't tell her of Mother's prophecy. She might think Mother is a little bit crazy.

Princess leans towards me. 'Tell me, Azari, do you know this autumn smell?'

'Fried food?'

She hoots with laughter. 'Outside. The smell *outside*. People here a *long* time talk about the smell of autumn in the air, but I don't know this autumn smell. Do you know it?'

I shake my head.

Princess stands up. 'Come with me. We will find this smell together, my friend.'

It seems a foolish thing to do but I follow her anyway, through the hall, past the baby buggies, scattered toys and random shoes. The front door stands open as usual. A couple of dark-skinned women talk on the concrete step.

'Hello, ladies,' Princess says.

It's almost dark out. Cold and fresh. I breathe it in. It's my first time outside today and I'm sorry now I didn't run when the day was bright and the sky clear. And now I'm outside with no jacket because Princess wants to smell autumn. My fingertips and nose are already chilly and there she is in her sunshine yellow dress and headscarf. Meri's words pop into my head: *you mad*!

'Are you not freezing?' I say.

'Good Irish air.' Princess laughs. 'It makes me feel *alive*.'

We walk down the driveway, away from the lights and voices of the Centre. Two boys fighting over a bike missing a wheel stop to stare at us. Under tall trees, the shadows are black and the mist makes everything ghostly. The ground is littered with leaves and tree nuts and broken twigs. Plastic bags. Old coffee cups.

Princess tramps across the damp grass, a yellow beacon glowing in the dark. She sniffs the air. 'What do you smell Azari?'

'Rotting leaves. Cold. Damp. Smoke.'

'*That's* the autumn smell? Rotting leaves? Cold and smoke?' she laughs, a hearty laugh that warms me. 'Not so good, eh? But it's good under here, isn't it? You know, the cold air on my skin. Tall trees. Gold leaves. Something magic is here. Something sweet in the air. It makes me *alive*.'

She puts emphasis on the word 'alive', so it jumps out of the dark like her yellow dress. Except it's Hallowe'en: the dead are awake, and Mother's prophecy is coming true tonight.

'Do you hear me?' she asks. 'Listen. Feel. See.'

Silhouettes of black trees. Soft light from the Centre. Cold sharp air. This is autumn. This is Ireland. Princess is right: there is something magic here.

'I hear you,' I say.

'*That* must be the autumn smell they talk about, Azari. The magic of being *alive* to this!'

We stand quietly beneath the dripping trees and soak up the stillness.

There's shouting. Engines. Sounds in the distance. Bright lights.

'Someone's at the gates.' I duck down. Squint beneath the branches.

The Centre gates are out of sight, around the bend of the driveway. The shouting is louder. It's not random; it's organised – like chanting. We stand in the darkness beneath the ghostly trees, Princess and me. We listen and wonder. People have come through the gates. They're coming up the driveway. Bright beams cut through the gloom.

'Torches,' I say.

Princess peers too. 'And cars.'

Everything is so much darker now. What little light was left has seeped away and the sky is black. Even though we're only two minutes from the Centre, I'm nervous.

'We should go back,' I say. Mother's warning echoes in my head: *The dead are out. Something bad is happening tonight.*

Chapter 13

By the time Princess and I get back to the main door, people outside are listening to the shouting, watching the lights. All chatter stops as the new arrivals come into view, marching up the driveway, raised voices joined together. They shine torches on their signs and banners. White clouds of breath hang in the air above them, like baby ghosts. Their dogs bark and yap, straining on leads.

The Centre manager appears at the front door. 'Inside now! We're locking up.'

'What's happening?' one man asks.

'I'm not moving,' says a woman sitting on the smoking seat.

'Have it your own way,' the manager shouts. 'We're locking the door now.'

Memories flood back of a rowdy crowd dragging my sister home, spitting and kicking. My heart beats hard. Tears prick my eyes.

Princess takes my arm. 'You OK?'

'I'm OK.'

'Let's go in.'

The woman from the smoking seat hurries in behind us.

'Shut and double-lock it,' the manager tells staff. 'Slide the bolts.' He picks up the phone as Mother comes out of the canteen.

'Your prophecy?' I say.

'My ghosts have been trying to tell me.' She grips my hand as the hall fills with curious residents.

'Get upstairs,' says the manager. 'TV room and canteen are closed.'

People grumble and give out. Most don't leave the front hall. It's crowded and noisy. Mother and the Farooqs, Meri, Princess and I cluster with everyone, staring out the big windows. The talking dies down. Even the manager stops shouting. Everyone listens to what's going on outside. Chanted words are clearer now:

> *What do we want?*
> *COMMUNITIES!*
> *When do we want them?*
> *NOW!*

Over and over they repeat it in rhythm with a drum beat. Behind the marchers, headlights from a line of cars shine blinding bright in the darkness. They manoeuvre around the protestors, revving and blasting their horns. Car lights shine on the placards:

Our town says NO!
Find Another Solution
NO Direct Provision here
Migrants, go home!

The marchers are all wearing Hallowe'en masks. I've seen them for sale in town: hideous zombies. Monsters. Bloodied clowns and witches. My skin crawls.

'The dead walk among us,' Mother whispers.

They hold sticks and branches, long planks of wood, boards. There's a pause in the shouting and a drum bangs three times. Everything stops. A single voice leads the crowd.

Communities? Communities?

YES! YES! YES!

Compounds? Compounds?

NO! NO! NO!

'The gardaí are on the way,' says the manager, his voice startling me. 'You can't be here. You're a fire hazard. Go on – clear off! Up to your rooms.'

Families and kids head upstairs. Mr and Mrs Farooq gather up their three children and leave the hall. I stay with Princess and others to watch as the crowd outside pull more planks and wood from the cars. Heap them on the gravel. Shadowed figures run under the trees to break branches and collect twigs to add to the heap. A lighter is set to the wood. Small flames flicker to life. Lick the tinder. The blaze grows higher, fanned by the breeze. The crowd cheers and shouts. Wood crackles. The snapping fire glows on leering masks and dancing monsters.

'Let's go,' I say to Mother when the bangers and firecrackers start.

Meri isn't in our room.

I open our window wide and poke my head out, but can't see the crowd or the bonfire: our room is at the side of the building. Firelight and shadows flicker across the grass where Princess and I stood earlier. The smoky air is full of chanting and drum beats, the crackle of the bonfire, the pop and whizz of firecrackers. Sometimes a gust of wind whisks bright sparks into the high branches and the night sky.

'Remember Father burnt the field to find Sharnaz?' I say.

'Shut the window, Azari.'

A blue light flashes down by the gates. The single whoop of a siren. 'The gardaí are here.'

'Shut the window.'

The shouting gets louder. Cheering and jeering as the gardaí arrive. The blue light goes out. Car doors slam. Voices get quieter but don't stop. The bonfire burns on. I wait, but can't see what's happening.

I shut the window.

We get ready for bed. Say our prayers. Settle down.

When fireworks start popping again, I know the gardaí have left. The flicker of the bonfire dances across the ceiling, then dies down. Cars start up and drive off.

I'm asleep when Meri comes in, flicking on the main light as if she has the room to herself. She roots in her bags. Rustles and mooches. Outside, voices still chant. Firecrackers fizzle and pop.

.   .   .

I wake again when the room is in darkness. Meri and Mother snore. There's no chanting or bangers. No flickering firelight. I'm just falling back asleep when I hear footsteps tread softly across the gravel beneath our window. I freeze. Listen.

I slide out of bed. Peer into the night. Two dark shapes creep along the side of the building, beneath where I stand. A security light flickers on: a skeleton and a grinning clown duck into the shadows. There's a brief flicker of light where they stand. Glass shatters. A vivid flash. The clown and the skeleton take off, pelting along the side of the Centre. Their footsteps race across the gravel and then they're gone.

I open the window a crack. There's a soft rushing noise from the broken window. Orange flames flicker below. Something smashes. This time, it's no Hallowe'en bonfire.

I whip around and shake Mother from her sleep.

'Fire! There's a fire downstairs!'

I stumble through the dark, groping my way. Switch on the main light. It's dazzling. Confusing. I squint. Shake Mother. She sits up, groggy.

'Sharnaz, is that you?'

I grab her coat, throw it over her shoulders. Pull back the bed clothes.

'Come on, get up! Get up!'

Meri grumbles and shouts at me; words I don't understand in her own language.

'Get up, Meri!' I shout. 'Fire!'

She stumbles from the bed. We hurry onto the landing, Meri falling and tripping over her own feet. Downstairs, glass shatters. There's a mighty whooshing sound. The canteen is full of wooden tables. Plastic chairs. Food for a hungry fire. Everyone is sleeping. They have to get out. How do I wake them?

'Fire! Fire!' Meri shouts. She bangs on doors but it's not enough.

The smell of smoke is strong now. Objects fall and break down below. Crackling. Popping. I look for the red break-glass unit we learned about in school. Smash it with the palm of my hand. Fire alarms scream through the Centre, enough to wake the dead. Bright lights switch on everywhere. There's a heartbeat's delay, then people tear open doors. Look onto the landing. Shout out.

'Fire!' I yell.

.   .   .

I help Mother down the stairs. Behind us, Meri curses or swears or prays in her own language.

People rush from rooms now, pounding down from bedrooms on higher levels. There's screaming and shouting. The staircase is crowded and noisy.

I hurry to the front door. Throw the latch, but it's double-locked from earlier. It won't open! The fire alarm hammers through my head. People crowd into the hall, shouting for help, looking for a way out.

'The kitchen!' I shout. 'Back door.'

I run down the back hall, past the locked canteen, and burst into the kitchen. Thick black smoke seeps beneath the canteen doors. It whirls in the air as we rush past. I'm coughing. Eyes watering. There's that other smell too: the one from the burning bush. Petrol!

The back door is chained shut. Bolted with a padlock.

'Here, Azari!' Meri shouts.

She's found emergency escape doors! Hands grip the cold metal bar. Wrench it down. The double doors fly open and we're out, pouring into the cold October night. Dozens of men, women and children, gasping, shouting, crying, calling for friends, family. I'm holding Mother. I grab Meri's arm. Drag them farther away. Together, we make our way onto the wet grass, freezing under my bare feet. We run under the dark trees. I only stop when we're a good distance from the building. Mother is breathless. Gasping. Coughing. She drops to the wet ground to catch her breath. Meri sits too.

'Are you OK?' I ask Mother. 'Can you breathe?'

She nods. Waves her hands that she's OK.

'Princess?' I shout into the night. I search the people around me. Peer into shadowed faces. 'Fiza?'

'Stay here,' I tell Mother.

'I stay with her,' Meri says and I nod. Smile gratefully at her.

I push my way through the crowd, tripping. Stumbling. Searching. 'Princess? Fiza? Mrs Farooq?'

Someone shouts my name.

'I'm here, girl.' And there's Princess, weaving through the confusion, her tall figure easy to spot. She has her two roommates with her, dazed and confused. Fiza appears next to me, carrying her baby sister wrapped in a fleece. She looks frightened, her face streaked with dirt. The baby is screaming.

'You OK?' I ask.

She nods, eyes full of tears.

'Where's your family?'

She points. They're all there, shivering in their nightclothes. Mrs Farooq is rocking a frightened toddler. I grab Fiza's hand, and with the Farooqs, Princess and a couple of others, weave my way back to Mother and Meri. We stay close together, looking at the burning building. People from the top floors scramble down the rusting staircases fixed to the walls. Red and orange flames lick the wooden windows. Black smoke billows through shattered glass. The alarm rings shrill and loud, and over it, fire engine sirens cut through the night air.

'That alarm would wake the dead,' I say to Mother.

'No need,' she says. 'They're already here.'

A fleet of fire engines, ambulances and garda cars arrive, filling the driveway with flashing blue lights, shouting and confusion. Firefighters storm the building, searching rooms, putting out the fire, checking everyone is safe. The firefighters climb long ladders from the fire engines to spray foam through broken windows. Gardaí move among us, taking names and room numbers. Checking family groups and roommates, asking who we share with, who we can account for. Ambulance workers treat the injured, driving off into the night with sirens blaring. We sit on the wet grass, shaking with cold, watching the activity. Mother and I hug each other close, teeth chattering.

Eventually, the gardaí bring everyone to hospital by car and ambulance, even if we're not hurt. We crowd into the warm waiting area. Most of us are in shock, shivering in our nightclothes. Barefoot. Hospital staff give us cups of sweet tea, hand out bundles of blankets, towels. Doctors and nurses check us over. Bring some people away for treatment. Gardaí talk to everyone, ask questions. Write down what we say.

It's only then the terror and fear swallow me up. We could've died. Every one of us could've been burnt up. If we hadn't managed to get out, if the emergency doors had been chained, if I hadn't heard the skeleton and the clown outside on the gravel, none of us might be here now. I feel sick and faint. I can't stop trembling even though I'm wrapped in a warm blanket.

'You look terrible,' Princess says.

'I feel sick.'

'Take some tea,' she urges me.

I sip hot sweet tea and immediately vomit into a bin. Mother spreads a blanket for me to lie down. Then we're left for hours, lying on the floor or sitting on rows of plastic seating. Parents unfold blankets to settle their children. Meri, Mother and Princess sit, bleary-eyed and exhausted. Fiza and Mrs Farooq sleep on the floor with the two little Farooqs. Mr Farooq spends his time looking for an official to talk to. When no-one answers his questions and he's told to sit down, he wakes his sleeping wife to complain to her. I doze a little. Think over what happened. What if I hadn't heard the footsteps? What if we had been asleep?

It's daytime when a garda comes to talk to us. I sit up, give him our names, room number, family group.

'The alarm was triggered on your floor,' he says. 'When did you hear it?'

'She ringed alarm!' Meri announces, leaning towards the garda. 'Azari woke. Woke me. Woke everyone. Good thing, yes?' She smiles broadly at me, slaps my shoulder.

I'm nervous. Maybe I wasn't allowed to touch the alarm. Was it for staff only?

'Did you set it off?' the garda asks.

I nod.

'How did you know? What happened?'

I tell him what I saw. The skeleton. The grinning clown. The flash. The flickering light. He asks me lots of questions, writes it all down.

'Am I in trouble?' I ask.

He shakes his head. 'Not at all – you're a guardian angel. We'd be facing a massive tragedy if you hadn't hit that alarm.'

'It wasn't wrong?'

'Wrong?' he smiles at me. 'It was great. Dozens of people are alive today because of your quick thinking.'

Some time after the garda has moved on, more gardaí arrive with bags of takeaway food for everyone.

'Get some food into you,' Mother says. 'It'll help with the shock.'

I don't know what time of day it is. It doesn't feel like lunchtime, but it's strange to be handed chips, milkshakes, burgers, and Coke for breakfast. I didn't realise how hungry I was and feel a lot better once I've eaten. We were all fading after our frightening night, but the food revives us. Little kids wake up and get excited. Mums and dads smile through their tiredness.

There's another surprise that afternoon when staff from the department store in town arrive with bulging bags of track-suits, jogging bottoms, warm sweatshirts, socks. Every one of us gets a whole outfit. We eagerly pull the new clothes over our flimsy nightwear.

'They're warm and cosy,' Mother says when I laugh at her in jogging bottoms.

Princess looks different without her usual vivid dresses and elaborate head-scarves. Her hair – normally covered with bright fabric – is pinned tightly to her head. Her face is drawn, bare of make-up.

It's evening when gardaí return to take us away in our family groups.

'Where to?' Princess asks for all of us. The whole waiting room falls silent to hear the answer.

'Local hotels and B&B's,' says the garda in charge. 'It's only temporary until we sort everything out and know what's happening for you. Somewhere safe to rest and recover.'

'What about our belongings?' Mr Farooq asks. 'Our clothes? Everything we own?'

'That'll take longer,' says the garda. 'The building hasn't been declared safe yet. It's also a crime scene. It'll take us a while to sort out belongings, return everything to you. We'll get in touch with each family group as we work through every-thing.'

'We can't wear these clothes until then,' Mr Farooq says.

He looks funny in a tracksuit. He normally wears *shalwar kameez*, like my father.

'We're doing everything we can, sir,' the garda says. 'This is an operational nightmare. We're organising accommodation, food, and clothing for over fifty people who've lost everything. On top of that, we've several seriously injured victims and an arson attack to investigate. It'll take time.'

But Mr Farooq is not giving up. 'And how do I feed and clothe my family while you take your time?'

The garda is annoyed. 'I know you're tired and in shock, sir, but if you wait, we'll get everything sorted in a few days.'

Mother and I are brought by garda car, with a smiling black family we don't know, to a B&B in town. We're given a cosy room only for the two of us, our own bathroom, a television and fresh clean bedding. There's no black mould across the walls. The shower is hot. No clumps of hair block the plughole.

When we arrive, the owner serves us tea and homemade scones with jam. 'It's only shocking what's after happening to you. And to think there's that kind of racism in this town. Who would've thought?'

I could tell her of racism every day, but it might get between her and her sleep. I say nothing. After hot showers, Mother and I are in bed early. We sleep through the night.

It's only the next morning I remember everything I've lost in the fire. My running gear: trainers, leggings, running shorts. Phone. Schoolbooks. All our clothes. Our application papers. My written story.

'Do you think they're all burnt up?' I ask Mother.

'If they are, we'll get more,' Mother says. 'It's more important we're safe.'

'What about our clothes from home – the ones we wore when we left? We can never get others, Mother. They're our only link.'

Mother's not as upset as I am. 'They're only clothes, Azari. They were old. Worn. Not so important. My link to home is in my heart.'

. . .

The garda was right: after a few days, things start to get sorted. We're given a special allowance for replacement clothes, toiletries, food, other items we might need. We buy nightclothes, undergarments, fleece jackets. The B&B gives us a full breakfast on real plates every day – much better than in the Centre – and we get a takeaway in the evenings at whatever time suits us, and definitely not at half past six. We choose the food we want and *never* go for Irish fried food. It's fun to try every takeaway café in town – Italian, Thai street food, Indian, Chinese, Greek. We like the Indian food best because it's closest to home. We order the spiciest dishes from the menu to eat in our room, watching television.

The fire is all over the news. Videos of the burnt-out building. Smoke-blackened walls. Smashed windows. Scorched grass. The walls have been sprayed with more giant red letters, spelling out words from the placards: 'Go home!' 'NO Direct Provision here.' 'Our town says NO!'

Mother's shocked. 'Did that happen after the fire?'

Black people and white people are interviewed on television. Refugees against politicians. Legal aid people against protestors. I look out for Sheila and Liz but don't see them. They argue about housing for asylum-seekers. Rights. Freedom of choice. Local reactions to Direct Provision centres. Too many foreigners in small towns. Too few houses. Not enough jobs. Mother wants to know what they're saying. I translate for her. Eight people were injured in the fire. Most are minor injuries, two critical, one serious. After a few nights of the same programmes, it gets too much. We find another channel where very big people compete with each other to eat less and exercise more.

Gardaí arrive at the B&B to ask me again about what happened on the night. I don't have anything more to tell them, but they want me to go over it again anyway. They ask questions about that entire evening: where we were, who I was with. What time the fire started. Who I saw. They tell us we'll be notified when they have any news about our belongings and about our accommodation.

I miss talking to Princess, to Robert, to Fiza. Even Meri at times. I wonder how they're doing. Where they are. I hope Fiza is staying with someone she can talk to and not only her family. I can't message anyone. Robert doesn't even know I'm OK.

'Do you want a new phone?' Mother asks.

'There's no point,' I say. 'I don't have their numbers. They won't know mine.'

The B&B is an easy walk to town, so I walk to the library to see if Fiza or Robert are there. No Fiza, no Robert, but the librarian smiles and nods.

'I'm sorry about what happened,' she says. 'Shocking alto-gether.' She reaches under the counter, takes out an envelope. 'Your friend comes by every day. The boy with bleached hair. He left this for you.'

I almost snatch the envelope from her, my heart tumbling with happiness. Robert came here! To ask for me.

'Thank you,' I say, and retreat to the far corner of the library. The note is short. I smile when I see it's addressed to Az – he's the only one who calls me this.

Hey Az, that's all crap. Don't know where u r but hope ur ok. Ur not giving up running cos of this. No xcuses. I'll call in at 4 every day till I catch u. R.

I go back to the library at four and there he is, a big happy grin on his face when he sees me.

'You OK?' he says.

'I'm OK.' I'm shy all of a sudden.

'That's where you lived, isn't it?'

Robert and I never spoke about where I lived. He never asked, which made me happy, and I never told him, because I was sick of seeing the change in people's eyes when they learned I was – am – in Direct Provision. But it seems he's known all along and I'm fine with that.

'Yeah, that's where I lived.'

We sit on the chairs and talk and talk. It's different than our usual chats when we're running. It's like we're trying to catch up with each other as fast as we can about everything that happened over the last few days. So much to talk about. There's an urgency to our questions and answers as though there's not enough time. His concern for me is comforting.

'I tried messaging you loads of times. I even rang, but couldn't get through,' he says.

'I left my phone behind in the rush to get out. Sorry.'

'Doesn't matter once you're OK. Was it scary?'

'I thought I was going to die. Smoke and flames everywhere. All these mad crashing sounds. We were coughing and choking. They had the front door locked.'

I'm reliving it again. How frightening it was. The panicked feeling rises in me, even though I'm safe. I rub my throat. Take a deep breath.

'I didn't know if you were safe,' Robert says.

'It was like the end of the world.'

'I thought maybe you were in the hospital.'

'We were taken there for a check-up.'

'And your ma?'

'She's fine too.'

'And that other girl – the young one?'

'Fiza? She's OK but I don't know where she's staying.'

'What's going to happen now?'

'Don't know. Everyone's in different places. We're staying in a B&B in town. I think they're trying to sort stuff out.'

'Will they move you?'

'Like – another town? Another centre?' I'm shocked at this. It never occurred to me we might be moved. I thought we'd stay here. 'Will they not move us back when the Centre is fixed up again?'

'That'll take for ever. And after the fire n all, it might not be used for … for …' he trips up a bit. 'Is refugees the right word?' he says at last. His face pinks up.

'Refugees is fine,' I say.

'Yeah well … refugees then.'

I don't want to move to another town. I want to stay here. I want to keep running with Robert. To be close to Princess and Fiza. I don't want to start all over again in yet another centre. Another school. Another life.

Chapter 14

After the midterm break, I go back to school, even though I don't have schoolbooks or copies or even a uniform. It feels weird walking to school from the B&B in leggings and a sweatshirt. No bus to get, no grumpy Seán, no half hour drive. Mother even comes to the door of the B&B to wave me off, like it's our own home. It's a good feeling.

There's a school assembly on the first day, which is unusual. All the teachers are seated on the stage in the hall. The principal has a whole speech prepared, all about the arson attack on the Centre and the Hallowe'en protest march and graffiti on the burnt-out building and poor injured people still in hospital. She talks about the fine students in our school who live in the Centre. Even though she doesn't name us, the nine of us in Black School might as well have flashing signs above our heads. Everyone in my class turns to look at me. They whisper and point.

The principal means well. She's being kind, but I'm mortified. My face burns. I want to curl up and die as she talks about tolerance and acceptance and the richness of diversity and different backgrounds and racism and inclusivity. It's like she's telling the whole school the story of my life. Making them *see* me. Making them feel sorry for me. I wish I was anywhere but here.

After assembly, we file back to our classrooms. People go out of their way to be extra friendly. I've never had so many girls look at me before. So many girls say hello to me and smile and mutter about me as I pass them on the school corridor. I don't know where to look. I wish the principal hadn't made such a big deal about what's going on. I'm used to being invisible. To hardly existing. Now, it's not possible. I've been catapulted to everyone's attention and there's no more hiding. I'm sure the other Centre girls are feeling the same as me, but none of them are in my year, so I don't have anyone to talk to about it.

I see the bunch of girls who've been horrible to me. For the first time, they don't look at me or say anything. Instead, they look embarrassed, clustered in a little knot. They turn away from me as I pass.

Relief washes over me when I see Emer's familiar face among all the students milling around. She grabs me on the corridor. Drags me into the nearest toilets.

'What the hell was that all about in assembly?' We both laugh. 'Stupid old goat making a holy show of the lot of you! She deserves a gold medal for being eejit of the year. Does she think you've no feelings? I was dying of embarrassment for you! Are you OK?'

'Just glad it's over. I didn't know where to look.'

'I'm not surprised!'

Her words of support make me feel a lot better.

'I still have to get through the rest of the day,' I say to her.

'Well good luck with that! Rather you than me.'

We head out of the toilets.

'Catch up later in the week.' And she's gone.

On the desk in my classroom sits a set of brand-new schoolbooks to replace the burnt ones: English, maths, geography, history. New pens and pencils in a zip-up pencil case. Even a new schoolbag.

'Your classmates got them for you,' the teacher says. She's smiling so widely, her face must be ready to split in two.

I'm scarlet as I mutter thanks.

The girls smile and nudge each other as they watch me lift my books down. Pull out my chair. Take my seat. I'm doing the same things I've done since I started in the school, but today, everything I do is extra special. Everything I do has lots of meaning and is worth watching. The teacher smiles and smiles. Her eyes are nearly brimming over with tears of sympathy.

This school day can't end soon enough.

. . .

The gardaí deliver five black bin-bags of clothes and belongings to the B&B. Mother has them emptied over the beds and is sorting them when I get back from school. I didn't know we even owned so much. It turns out, we don't.

'Half of these aren't even ours,' Mother says, holding up men's shirts and trousers. 'Must be Meri's.'

'Meri doesn't have men's clothes.' I grab a bundle of them. 'They're soaked through! And they stink.' I open the window. 'Must be the smoke.'

Most of the clothes are destroyed from water and smoke. We fill three bin-bags with wet, blackened clothes we don't own, and leave them outside. We rinse out the clothes we're keeping, arrange a few items on the shelves. There's not much.

'Is that all we have?' Mother says. 'Our whole lives?'

'There's loads of stuff missing,' I say.

'Must be with another family in some other B&B,' Mother says.

·   ·   ·

When we get our half-day on Wednesday, I walk to the girls' primary school behind the convent. Stand outside the gates until the kids are let out. I'm not sure which door to wait at, but quickly spot the senior classes pouring out at one end of the playground. I'm watching and waiting. Hoping I haven't missed her among all the bobbing heads. Finally, I spot her black hair and brown face.

'Fiza!' I shout.

She whips her head up straight away. The grin that spreads across her face is enough to make my heart flip. She races across the playground, breathless and excited.

'What are you doing here?' she says.

To my astonishment, she grabs me. Hugs me tight. I hug her back, happy to see her.

'I miss you,' she says. 'I thought I'd never see you again.'

'Miss you too. I went to the library to look for you.'

'Me too! Must've been on different days.'

I'm pleased we both tried to find each other.

'Where are you staying?' I ask.

'A hotel up the town. Four families there but we don't know the others.'

'Have you seen Meri? Princess?'

'Nobody. My mother misses talking to your mother so much. She's no-one except Father and he's being awful: complaining to anyone who'll listen. He doesn't even have his phone to distract him. I was never so happy to go back to school.'

'And the babies?'

'They're fine. Up to mischief. It's much harder being in one room – there's no outside area or TV room to bring them to.'

We walk up the town to Fiza's hotel, chatting the whole way. It's great to catch up with her. I tell her where I'm staying, fill her in on school and meeting Robert.

'We only got half our stuff back,' she says. 'Mother had to throw most of it out because it smelt so bad. I've no phone so I couldn't message you.'

'I've no phone either.'

'Maybe we could webtext?' She laughs when she sees my face. 'It's easy. I'll set it up for you on the library computer, though we'll have to do it before the weekend cos they're moving everyone to new centres next week.'

'That's what Robert said too. But so soon! Do you know where you'll be going?'

Fiza shakes her head. 'Don't think anyone does. Father's been asking about it all week. Nobody seems to know.'

We arrange to meet the next day and I trail back to the B&B, happy I've seen her but miserable about moving on. What's worse is I can't even go for a run to clear my head because I've no running shoes or clothes.

We end up meeting in the library every day for the rest of the week. Robert joins us too. He's mad keen for us to go running on Saturday.

'But it's what we always do,' he complains when I say I can't.

'I've no running gear.'

'Leggings and a T-shirt are fine.'

'And what – bare feet?' I see him trying to come up with a funny comment about running and bare feet. I hold up my hand. 'Don't even say it.'

Fiza sets us up on webtext. Gives us a run down on the basics.

'My English spelling isn't good,' I tell her. 'Just warning you.'

'That makes two of us,' Robert says. 'And don't even get me started on my spelling in your language.'

.   .   .

The following week, things happen just as Fiza said. Nine of us in Black School drop to six – Miracle, Katya and Amira are gone. When the sisters Meetha and Mishra don't return, there are only four of us left. The resource teacher asks if we know where they've gone, but we've no idea.

I get back from school one afternoon and Mother tells me the black family have left.

'A garda car arrived and took them away,' she says.

'A garda car? Were they scared?'

Mother shakes her head. 'All smiles. Waving and shouting goodbye.'

When I meet Fiza in the library, she tells me two families in the hotel have gone. She doesn't look happy. 'We're being collected tomorrow.'

'Where are you going?'

'Don't know. I'll message you as soon as I find out.'

We hug tightly. Fiza is like my little sister now. Princess's words come to mind: *Let her into your heart a little. She's trying to find her place in this strange new world we find ourselves in.* I've let her into my heart a lot.

'I've already lost one sister,' I tell her. 'I'm not about to lose another.'

'You won't lose me.' She wipes away her tears. 'You're stuck with me now. I need someone who understands what it's like.'

'Be strong. And don't listen to your father all the time – it's *your* life, not his.'

'Now you sound like Princess!'

·   ·   ·

The owner of the B&B knocks on our door that evening.

'Someone asking for you at the front door,' she says. 'I didn't want to let her in without checking with you.'

'Probably Fiza,' I say to Mother.

But it's not Fiza.

'Well now, Azari-*Nike*, you've been a *difficult* young lady to track down!' a familiar voice sings out.

'Princess!'

I can't believe it. We hug tightly. I bring her to our room to talk. She fills the whole room with her presence, her bright orange dress and headscarf with pink and yellow zigzags. She looks like herself again, unlike when I last saw her in the hospital. Her glossy hair is piled high and as she's telling us her news, her hands wave through the air, silver bangles jangling on her wrists, long nails polished in bright orange.

'I've been staying in a B&B the *far* side of town on my own. *Nobody* else from the Centre is there and I'm beginning to think they want to *hide* me away or something. Do you think I could get *any* information about where you are? Seems like it's a state *secret* and everyone was spirited away except me. I couldn't find *nobody*.'

'How did you find me?'

'I told the gardaí I had *given* you my application papers for safe keeping and I *had* to find you to get them back before you were shipped off to *Mars* and I'd never see you again.'

I can just imagine Princess making the gardaí hand over the name of our B&B. 'Did you get your belongings back?'

'Did I *what*? I got back six dresses I had left in the prefab dryer and *that is it*! *Nothing* else has come back to me. Thank *heaven* I washed those six dresses the day before Hallowe'en or I'd be going around in some awful baggy tracksuit. What about you?'

I tell her about our belongings, about school, about Robert and Fiza, about going to a new Centre. Princess shakes her head.

'I'm *refusing* to go to another new Centre,' she says. 'I already told them no. I can't do that any more. It's worse than prison. Eats the soul from a person and leaves only a dried-out shell. We arrive here looking for help and protection, every one of us tormented and traumatised. Six months later, they have us institutionalised and damaged and going crazy. No, girl, I'm done with Direct Provision.'

'What are you going to do instead? Where will you go?'

'I've been doing a *lot* of thinking and planning while I've been in that B&B. I have cousins in *Canada*. They tell me it's *good* over there. Open and accepting. I've decided to give it a try. I'm leaving Ireland. I *can't* put up with this system any more.'

I don't know where Canada is but I'm not surprised Princess is leaving this country. She writes down her email address for me.

'You better keep in touch and tell me when you've *qualified* for the Olympics. I'll be cheering for you, girl.'

It's late when she leaves. I walk her to the front door. Saying goodbye to people is hard. First Fiza. Now Princess.

'Don't think of it as goodbye,' she says. 'Think of it as missing each other until we meet again. And I'll definitely meet you again, Azari-Nike.'

The last I see of Princess is her tall figure as she walks up the road towards her B&B, her vivid pink, yellow and orange dress bright under the street light. I stand at the door in the dark, watching her silhouette until she fades into the night and I no longer see her colours.

.   .   .

A garda arrives on Friday evening with more belongings.

'You're moving to a new Centre next week,' she says. 'We'll be collecting you Monday afternoon. We'll drive you there. Make it a bit easier after everything that's happened.'

'Where is it?'

'Couple of hours away. They've it all ready for you. You'll even be there in time for dinner.'

'Anyone else we know going there?'

'I'm not supposed to tell you.' She winks at me. 'But let's have a little look.' She pulls out a list of names and centres, scans down it. 'Nope. Only you two going from here. Nice to have a fresh new start, eh?'

Once she's left, we upend the bin-bag. My trainers and some schoolbooks tumble out, scorched and stinking of smoke. A hairbrush. A cloth bag of bangles. One of my early letters from the IPO, but no other papers or documents. The IPO. My heart feels heavy when I see the letter. The process of applying for international protection isn't over. I have to let Liz know my new address, and hope it's not so far that I won't be able to meet her. Will I have to find yet another legal aid person? The darkness edging at the corner of my mind begins to creep in on me, like clouds before the monsoon. I take a deep breath. Put it out of my head for now.

I've more important things to think about now I have my running shoes back.

My phone and charger are also in the bag. The screen is cracked, the sleek pink surface chipped. I plug it in. The little red light flickers for a few seconds, then stays steady.

'It's charging!'

Even with a broken screen, I manage to message Robert to see if he's up for a run tomorrow. He gets back straight away:

Defo. C u 2moro.

Saturday morning can't come quick enough.

'You get to choose the route,' Robert says when we meet at the library.

'That's always been your job! I don't know where to go.'

'Let's mix it up today.' He grins at me. 'What about the old train track, but in reverse?'

'Heading out of town instead?'

We start off by the river. It feels so good to be out running again, even if I am wearing smoke-blackened trainers and it might just be my last run with Robert. A fresh breeze blows my hair back and cools my face. There's been so much happening, I need this run to clear my head. To slow my racing thoughts. I've been doing a lot of thinking since the garda told us where we're going.

'Will we be able to keep up our Saturday runs?' I say as we cool down at the end.

He whips his head round. 'I thought you were moving far away? Like a hundred kilometres or something? That you couldn't … That we wouldn't …' He trails off.

I shrug. 'I think it's only a couple of hours away. I'm sure I can get a bus. If you'd be OK changing our runs to a Saturday afternoon, maybe we could still meet up sometimes?'

A rush of warmth floods me when I see the enormous grin spread across his face.

'Now you look like an eejit,' I tell him.

'You could change in my house after,' he says. 'So you don't have to get the bus back all sweaty and stinky. Maybe get a bite to eat at mine first.'

'Will ya hang on there, bud!' I laugh. 'Let's just see if it'll work first.'

'Oh, it'll work.' He nods his head so much it looks like it's about to fall off. 'We'll make it work.'

So then there's no need for us to say goodbye, which is a huge relief because I was dreading it. No need for hugging or long farewells.

'I'll get in touch as soon as we're settled,' I tell him.

'Or maybe even before that,' he grins.

'Maybe even before that.'

I turn and walk towards our B&B.

'Hey, Az?' Robert yells after me.

I turn back.

'To the moon and back,' he shouts.

. . .

We're collected on Monday afternoon. I don't go to school that day. We get our stuff together, pack our bin-bags in the boot of the garda car and leave town. It's only then I remember Meri.

I never found out what happened to her or where she's gone. She's like most of the other people in the Centre: scattered around the country to new centres.

Mother reaches for my hand. Holds it tightly.

'What are your ghosts saying today?' I ask.

'Nothing.' She smiles. 'They're sleeping. It's a good sign. All is right.'

We pass the gates to the burnt-out Centre. I catch a glimpse of the scorched building. I hated it there, but I made friends. Friends I'll keep for ever.

And you still have me, Azari, Sharnaz whispers to me.

I haven't heard from her since the fire. 'Where have you been?'

You've had a lot on, I didn't want to distract you. But I'm here. I'll always be here.

'It's good to have you back,' I whisper.

The garda car swings onto the motorway and I smile to myself as I gaze out the window.

. . .

Some things about my new life in Ireland are difficult, but most are exciting. I have proper friends now who make me feel welcome. Who make me feel I belong. And it occurs to me for the first time that I too have my own ghost. Except mine doesn't foresee bad news; instead, she guides me and cares for me. And as I watch the Irish countryside slip past, I recall Robert's words after our run and my heart skips a beat: *To the moon and back, Azari.*

To the moon and back.

What Is Direct Provision?

Direct Provision was established in Ireland in 2000 and is the system of state-provided accommodation and other basic necessities to people seeking international protection. Under the Direct Provision system, people are accommodated across the country in communal institutional centres, mainly hostels, hotels and other accommodation owned and run by private companies for profit, paid for by the Irish government.

Direct Provision was designed as a short-term emergency measure to provide for the basic needs of people who are awaiting decisions on their applications for international protection. Instead, it has lasted more than 21 years.

People were meant to spend no longer than six months while their asylum application was processed. Instead, they are trapped, often for years, waiting for a decision about their futures. Many people have to stay in overcrowded conditions, sharing bedrooms and bathrooms with strangers, lacking dignity and privacy. These conditions are associated with declining physical and mental health, self-esteem and skills.

Direct Provision centres are often in isolated locations far from local communities. The isolation and hopelessness can damage physical and mental health and prevent people from restarting their lives once they are recognised as refugees.

Direct Provision is particularly difficult for families, children, young people, people who have experienced trauma, violence or torture, and other vulnerable people.

The system has raised major human rights concerns. The toll that it takes on its residents has been well documented by NGOs, legal practitioners, experts and international bodies, with the Ombudsman and the special rapporteur on child protection both calling on Ireland to abolish Direct Provision.

In 2021, more than 7,000 people lived in Direct Provision centres across Ireland, of whom over 2,000 were children.

Key Issues

Length of time: The average length of stay in Direct Provision is 24 months, with some residents having spent up to 10 or 12 years living in these conditions.

Profit: The majority of Direct Provision centres are managed by private contractors on a for-profit basis, on behalf of the Irish state.

Employment: Until February 2018, asylum seekers had no right to work in Ireland – unlike most EU member states. Restrictions still apply and the majority of people who live in Direct Provision centres have no right to access employment.

Education: People living in Direct Proivision have limited access to further and higher education.

Isolated locations: Some centres are located in rural areas, with limited transport options and support services.

Privacy and overcrowded living conditions: Residents live in shared accommodation, with single adults sharing rooms with up to eight people of different backgrounds and nationalities.

Food: Three meals are provided at set times each day; limited cooking facilities are available in a small number of centres. Complaints have been made regarding lack of variety and lack of nutritional options in the centres.

Standards and monitoring: The living conditions vary widely from centre to centre. There is little trust in the complaints procedure and limited publicly accessible information on complaints or transfer decisions. The existing inspection system focusses on health and safety issues and does not consider the social or emotional needs of residents.

Health: Physical and mental health issues among residents are very common. Asylum seekers are five times more likely to experience mental health issues and psychiatric conditions.

Children: Around 30% of Direct Provision residents are children. Children have been born and raised living in these conditions, the long-term developmental effects of which are still unknown.

The information above on Direct Provision was obtained from the following websites, where more information about campaigns and action to end Direct Provision can be found:

amnesty.ie/end-direct-provision

doras.org/direct-provision

irishrefugeecouncil.ie/listing/category/direct-provision

Acknowledgements

Run For Your Life started out as a conversation with Siobhán Parkinson and the team at Little Island Books about the story of a young person living in Direct Provision and the process of applying for asylum in Ireland. I would like to thank Siobhán, Matthew, Kate and Elizabeth for their prescience in publishing this book, and for their commitment to advocating for those in Direct Provision who might not yet have a voice of their own to tell their stories. Little Island has been a warm and friendly home for Azari's tale, and the book as it stands now is so much richer and stronger for Siobhán's expert eye and deft editing.

I would like to thank the illustrator and graphic designer, Wajeeha Abbasi, for the beautiful cover that incorporates influences from Azari's current and former life.

Thanks are due to Vukasin Nedeljkovic for taking the time to meet with me to speak of his experience in Direct Provision. Vukasin's digital records of Direct Provision Centres are preserved for the future on www.asylumarchive.com and in his book of the same name. The raw images are a stark reminder of the isolation and hopelessness of Direct Provision centres.

The Movement of Asylum Seekers in Ireland (www.masi.ie) is an independent platform for asylum seekers to join together in unity and purpose, seeking justice, freedom and dignity for all asylum seekers. MASI organised the powerful 'Voice of the Voiceless' conference for asylum-seekers at which young people – among others – spoke of their experience living in Direct Provision. Their compelling stories, personal insight, and strength of character impacted deeply on me. They deserve so much more, and I'm very grateful to have had the opportunity to listen.

Thanks to Debbie Thomas, author and all-round force for good, for her help and support in the early stages of the book, to Jody Clarke in UNHCR, and to publicist Peter O'Connell. And finally, my gratitude to Liz, Maria, Paul and Sandra, for their lasting friendship and for providing feedback, support, and guidance in so many ways – sometimes without even knowing it.

About Jane Mitchell

Jane Mitchell has written several books for children and young people which have won national and regional awards in Ireland and the UK, including the Bisto Book of the Year, Children's Books Ireland Merit Award, Reading Association of Ireland Merit Award, and Children's Choice award. Her books have been listed on the school curriculum in Ireland and Brazil. *A Dangerous Crossing*, which told the story of Syrian refugees, was shortlisted for the Irish Book Awards Children's Book of the Year in 2017, and also for the CBI Book of the Year Award in 2018, and has sold over 100,000 copies worldwide.